I0530734

DRAG

UNDIVIDED

Leigh Jarrett

This book is a work of fiction. The characters, incidences, and dialogue are drawn from the author's imagination and are not to be construed as real. Any resemblance to actual events or persons, living or dead, is entirely coincidental.

DRAG UNDIVIDED Copyright © 2023 by Leigh Jarrett. All rights reserved. No part of this book may be used or reproduced in any manner whatsoever without written permission, except in the case of brief quotations embodied in critical articles and reviews. All trademarks are the property of the respective owners.

Published by Steambath Press
An LJ M/M Romance

Paperback published September 2023
ISBN-13: 978-1-998008-19-3

Chapter One | Cole

Cole held the hot washcloth to his face, rubbed his eyes with it, and pulled it away, depositing the wet mess of makeup-stained cloth into the sink. He looked at his reflection in the mirror. Leaned forward and examined his eyes. They looked weary and bloodshot. It had been a long night last night. Two separate shows. He'd needed to run from one to the next. Luckily, they were only blocks apart but he'd been forced to dash through downtown Kelowna, BC in full drag in precarious heels. He'd had an entourage of gay men with him. It hadn't felt risky.

Even if it had been …

He had drunk far too much alcohol to care. People had a habit of buying the drag performers shot after shot and Cole never turned down a free drink. He'd nearly sprained his ankle last night when he'd stumbled on his platform heels while off stage because he was so drunk.

Tequila had been his shot of choice. The audience had obliged with the libation. Keeping them coming on stage all night long. He'd had his last one just before he left for the night after schmoozing with the crowds of people that had gathered in Kelowna's only gay bar.

He'd been propositioned by a gay couple but he hadn't felt up to a night of sex. It was a lot of work satisfying two or more people. Especially if they were a straight couple. Diving into pussy wasn't something he did very often. His technique wasn't great. They never seemed to care. Just having a drag queen in bed with them was enough excitement for whomever he was with.

Whatever their sexuality, the men were always primed to fuck him.

Often, he ended up stumbling around strange neighborhoods in drag at 3 am, waiting for a cab. He knew it was dangerous but the alcohol typically wiped out his fear.

Back at home last night, he barely managed to pull off his wig before he collapsed, kneeling in front of the toilet and reacquainting himself with his longtime friend, the white porcelain god.

Now his head was pounding and he still felt nauseous but he was due back at the bar in two hours for another show. It was 8 am. He'd booked himself in to perform at drag brunch.

Cole had to keep a tight schedule. This was his sole livelihood. He'd gone to school to be a special needs child educator and worked for years in the field, but things had gone haywire in the school system. Anti-gay protests were breaking out around the acceptance of LGBT rights in schools. Anti-SOGI tirades even happened in school district council chambers.

Protect the Children!

To fight back, Cole had picked up a gig doing Drag Storytime at the downtown library because he loved kids. He wanted them to grow up in a kind and accepting environment. The crowds attending were huge, but the protesters at storytime eventually figured out who Cole was in real life and had been relentless. He had been harassed at home and in the parking lot at work.

Six months ago, his drag personality social media page had been pulled down without notice, likely reported by the anti-gay, anti-drag protesters as being the page of a groomer pedophile.

It was complete and utter bullshit.

He'd decided he'd had enough and he'd quit his job at the

school he loved.

He lifted a shot of tequila to his lips. Hair of the dog along with two aspirin and an anti-nausea pill and he'd be right as rain. No one could ever accuse him of being anything less than fabulous. He had a reputation as one of the best drag performers in town and he was safeguarding it.

It had started ten years ago, his love of drag. It had been a dare to get up on his first stage. A local drag celebrity had become friends with him and was always commenting on the delicate and feminine traits of his face and his sharp wit. She'd finally convinced him to give it a go. She'd painted his face and lent him a costume. The effects he saw in the mirror alone had convinced him.

He was hooked.

He'd burst onto that stage like he was meant to be there. Not even three weeks after his amateur performance, he'd been pulled from the newbie circuit and given his own weekly spotlight.

Cole headed for his makeup table and sat himself down on the stool. The tools of his craft were laid out neatly on the plastic-covered surface. The makeup table was an antique passed down from his grandmother. She'd been incredibly supportive of his supplementary career choice.

He smoothed his hand across the surface of the table.

She'd been gone for years.

Cole lifted the purple glue stick and flattened his eyebrows down, sticking them to his face. Normally, he would have popped on a wig cap next, but he had no hair to speak of, except for the shadow of dark blond. He had decided to shave his head last week. It made life easier.

Next was his wide paint stick. He covered his eyebrows completely with it, blending what had been glossy purple and brown into the background of his forehead. He moved it to his beard areas and covered the constant dark shadow of his jawline and lip in the thick full-coverage makeup.

He used a sponge in all the crevices and blended that shit out, making his face look like a flat paintable canvas. And his neck. He'd been feeling washed out recently, plus it was summer, so he decided to *give himself a tan*. Cole took a darker cream contour stick and ran it along the outer edge of his face and down his neck, then blended it out, covering his entire face, neck, and shoulders—and his chest. He'd likely be wearing a costume that had dropped shoulders.

A cream blend stick in white was next. He painted a teardrop shape to cover his cheekbones, then used a second sponge to press it across his cheekbones and around his eyes. He blended the edges and set everything in place with a special powder.

He'd need to be well powdered to withstand the heat in the gay bar this morning. Summer was cooking. And it started early in the day. Okanagan temperatures could sky-rocket by 9 am.

He packed pure white eyeshadow on the hollows under his eyes. He'd need the illusion of health to counterbalance the dark circles that were now a permanent fixture. He blinked at himself in the mirror as he finished applying it. He almost looked normal.

Some dark powder was next to create a nice deep forehead contour, then along the bridge of his nose, drawing it out along the center. He powdered under his eyes and on his beard areas, and a little bit at the top angle of his jawline, and right in the center of his forehead.

The palette of his face complete, he turned to his eyebrows. He used ash-colored eyeshadow to start the shape of a new brow. He introduced a darker color with a smaller brush to give them more dimension, then switched to a liquid eyebrow liner to increase the number of eyebrow lines.

Black liquid eyeliner was next. Cole liked a thick cat-eye

effect. He painted one eye, then used the same eyeliner to carve a soft line along the top of his lid, and then blended it out with medium brown eyeshadow. He took a deeper brown and continued to create the definition.

Cole pulled out his eyeshadow palette and chose a silver glitter eyeshadow. He pressed a coating of it onto this eyelid. He used a touch of white eyeshadow just under his eyebrow, then added black liner under his eye, and blended it out with brown shadow.

He moved to the other eye and repeated the entire process. It was time-consuming but worth it. It gave his eyes a truly feminine look.

He gripped his makeup table and closed his eyes for a second as the room seemed to spin. It was possible he was still drunk from last night and he'd just added fuel to that.

Cole took a deep breath and went back to work. He curled his lashes, added some mascara, and then used tweezers to lift a false eyelash. He applied the glue and popped it on one eye and then repeated it for the other. He turned his head back and forth, looking at himself, blinking, fluttering the long lashes. Even he could admit, he was stunning. He picked up the liquid eyeliner and added some bottom lashes toward the inside of his eye to make up for the shortcoming.

Better.

His green eyes stared back at him.

He had to look away.

He blended his entire face with a large brush and then opened a light-colored powdered blush and used it on his cheeks, temples, and a small touch on the end of his nose. He used a highlighter just under the outside of his eyes and then created a soft line down the center of his nose.

Cole looked at his chest in the mirror. He added a little highlighter to emphasize the center of his chest to create some cleavage between his man-titties. He cupped his pecs with his hands and lifted them, imagining what it would be like to have actual breasts. Not that he wanted them. He was thrilled to be a gay man in a virile man's body. It was just a ponderance, breasts.

He added a warmer blush to his cheekbones, softening his face, and then a few soft dots of dark shadow across his cheeks and over his nose to create some natural skin texture. He dusted it all with a brush. Next were his lips. He used dark crimson lipstick liner to create a cupid's bow and then moved to below his lip to create an exaggerated lip. He filled in his lips with the lip liner.

He turned his head back and forth, then added a lighter color along the center of his lips. He topped it all off with a gloss. He sighed as he finished. He looked good overall.

Not like someone who was crashing and had only had 5 hours of sleep.

Cole went in search of the lavender blond wig that was straight-cut glamor all the way to his waist. He'd spent significant time with a straightening iron getting it completely flat. Usually, he had a stylist handle his wigs but he was broke at the moment. Family stuff.

He placed some double-sided tap along what would be his hairline, then pulled on the wig and set it in place with spray-on glue and a hairdryer.

His look was complete.

Trixie Lamour was born and ready to party.

He had to think about what outfit he was going to wear. With a skirt, he could go lightly tucked. With a bodysuit, he had to hide his cock completely.

He felt like punishing himself.

Bodysuit it was.

Cole went to the bathroom and used a razor to make sure he was shaved well enough that the tuck tape wouldn't have anything long to stick to. Outright pain wasn't on his agenda.

He made sure to empty his bladder. It would be hours until he could use the washroom again unless it was an emergency. He would not be having coffee this morning.

He kept his tucking supplies in the bathroom so he could use them in front of the mirror. He started by rolling some tubular gauze over his penis, twisted the gauze while it was halfway down then folded it over on itself and completed capping the tip of his cock.

Next came the tuck tape. Cole used specially designed tape in the shape of a pyramid with a long tail at the peak. He peeled away part of the backing paper and stuck the wide exposed sticky tape to his pubic area just above his shaft. Not his favorite part, but he reached between his legs from the back with one hand and pushed his testicles into the cavity they had descended from in utero. Then flattened his penis between his legs and held the entire thing in place.

He switched hands so he was holding everything from the front. He removed the rest of the backing paper and while pulling firm, he taped his penis in place, yanked the tape up between his butt cheeks, and pressed the thinner tape end to his skin at the small of his back.

He looked at himself in the mirror. If you didn't know better, you'd think he'd had his cock removed … and that would be a damn crying shame. He loved his cock. Loved when men sucked on it and deep-throated it. Loved fucking a guy's hole with it. Loved cumming all over himself.

The dirtier, the better. He loved it all.

His cock stirred, so Cole redirected his thoughts to unpleasant things to calm it down. He had a shit-load of paperwork to do. His dad had passed away three weeks ago, leaving everything to his mom and naming her as executor of his will. But his mom had dementia which meant Cole had to enact the power of attorney provision set up for his mom. Then move forward from there.

He had been named as the alternate executor of his dad's estate … so there was that. And then their house. His mom had been placed in long-term care four months back. With his dad gone, there was no one living there. Cole had to make a decision. Sell it or rent it out.

It was almost more stress than he could handle.

He looked at the racks of costumes clogging his living room. It was impossible to sit down anywhere anymore. Along with the racks of clothes were piles of shoes, shelves of wigs on mannequin heads, trays of jewelry, and an assortment of foam hips pads and silicone boobs.

Sometime in the last year, his collection had spilled out of his second bedroom into the main space. Sometime after his husband had given up on him and walked out of his life.

Spouting something about Cole being a drunken mess.

He wasn't wrong.

Cole chose his costume. It was covered in purple and silver sequins. It was heavy but it fit well. He pulled on his tights first and padded his hips slightly. He didn't like the overdone hips some of the girls sported. He liked a more natural effect. He shimmied the bodysuit into place and scratched his arms to bits as he fed them through the shoulder straps.

Costume in place, he grabbed a couple of silicone *chicken cutlets* and used them to fill out his outfit in the chest area and push up what little flesh he had on his pecs into a breast-like shape.

He scanned through his shoes. He didn't want a repeat of last night. He felt unsteady on his feet. He chose a pair of silver, sparkly, three-inch heels. They were safer than platform heels.

Cole looked at his phone. He had an hour. He should've eaten before getting ready. Now his stomach was objecting but he didn't want to mess up his lips. He snagged a boxed protein shake from the fridge, popped a straw in it, and drank the whole thing. That would have to do for now.

He rehearsed some of his ideas for banter with the crowd in his head. Mostly, it came naturally, spilling out of his mouth without much thought. He had to be careful at brunch, though. Entertaining a bunch of straight women, stagette parties, and straight couples—the bread and butter of drag brunch—was infinitely different from entertaining a club full of queers at night.

Not that the banter wouldn't become sexual. It always did with him. He liked to tease the shy ones. Elicit brash responses from the brave ones. And generally have everyone laughing.

It was a skill.

And Cole had it in spades.

No.

Trixie Lamour had it in spades. He just facilitated it.

It carried into his real life as well. He had a quick tongue that he used to keep everyone at bay. People never got to know the real Cole. The shy, sensitive Cole. The one with feelings.

The Cole who currently had the weight of the world on his shoulders.

Chapter Two | Noah

Noah closed the door of his office. He needed to be alone for a few minutes. The morning had been meeting after meeting. In the afternoon, he might be able to get the stacks of paperwork done. He had three probate files on the go. Plus his usual workload of will and power of attorney preparation. His week had been brutal. He was actually looking forward to the weekend.

He flipped open the wedding invitation on his desk. It had been unexpected. He hadn't talked to Debbie in years. She and her fiance, Naomi, had decided to host a wedding slash mini-high school reunion. The response had been well ... sparse because of the location.

The event was happening in the Kootenays in Kaslo, BC on an old farm of sorts near a deep glacier-fed lake surrounded by jutting mountaintops. Kaslo was a small town with a population of one thousand and forty-nine people that swelled in summer. The brides to be had rented a resort in the middle of a heavily forested area, away from any major civilization.

It was just what Noah needed. Time in nature. One of his favorite hobbies was camping. British Columbia had so much to offer when it came to campsites and varied landscapes. From rolling arid deserts to rugged Pacific coastlines to thick mountainous rainforests.

His phone dinged with a text message. His legal assistant, Carol, wanted him to fit in one last client for the day. The phone on his desk rang.

"Sorry," Carol said. "I promised a new client I'd get him in to see you today for an initial consult. I felt bad for him. He sounded really stressed out."

"Aren't they all?"

"Please, Noah. It won't take long."

"That's it for the day, though. I have work to do."

"I know. The files on my desk are becoming like the leaning tower."

"Send him in at 1:10. No earlier."

"Got it."

The line disconnected.

That extra ten minutes would give Noah time to organize his notebook after lunch. He liked to be on top of things. Notes on everything. All the facts clearly documented.

Much like his life, his work environment was regimented.

It meant he had less to worry about. He just needed to follow his routine every day. Step after step until he got to the end of his day. A day that often lasted late into the night. Being a lawyer meant having mountains of paperwork to get through on a regular basis.

Ted, a senior partner, popped his head into Noah's office. "What are you doing for lunch?"

"Not sure yet." Noah looked at his phone. 11:30. If he didn't go now, he wouldn't get back in time for his appointment. Lunch with a partner frequently meant a lot of shop talk. It could go on for hours and because you were with a boss, there was no rush to get back to the office.

He rose from his seat. "Rosie's?" Noah suggested. "I'm feeling like pasta."

"Perfect. They have some nice reds there."

The second thing about going for lunch with one of the partners, it often meant there would be alcohol involved. Noah didn't typically drink, but he could be pressured into a single glass.

He slipped on his suit jacket and followed Ted to the

elevator. They emerged onto the sunny sidewalk. They were going to walk. It was only two blocks from the office to the restaurant.

It was a hot summer day. Sweltering, in fact. The cocoon created by Noah's light woolen suit jacket became stifling. He realized too late that he should have left it in the office. He was going to end up with sweat stains under the arms of his crisply ironed white shirt. He tugged off his jacket, slung it over his shoulder, and yanked on the knot of his tie to loosen it.

The restaurant was soon in sight. Just a door and windows between other shops. A barber on one side. A sex shop on the other. Noah glanced in the window of the sex shop. There were male mannequins wearing black leather harnesses and females in slinky lingerie on display.

The sight of those harnesses in that window always made his cock stir.

Noah redirected his attention and held open the door of the restaurant for Ted. The cool air hit them immediately. It was glorious. Almost cold. Noah was glad of the reprieve from the heat.

They were led to a table.

The place probably hadn't been redecorated in forty years. Rosie's might have been the original tenant. The interior was all dark wooden spindles and forest-green walls. In complete contrast, the tablecloths were red and white checkers. It was gaudy but the food was good.

"9oz house red—two," Ted started their order.

"And a Caesar salad to start for me," Noah said.

Ted waved his hand at the server. "I'm fine with wine for now."

Noah flipped over the menu. He already knew what he wanted. Their individual lasagna was to die for. So much garlic, you tasted it for days. And the serving was large enough that he could take some home for dinner tonight. He'd be on the treadmill for hours to work it back off.

"So, how's your workload?" Ted asked.

"Bursting at the seams."

Ted grinned. "Good. I'm glad we brought you on."

"Thrilled to be part of the team."

Six months back, Noah had made the move from his family's small legal firm to Legatte, Cruiz, and McAllister. Noah had needed a change of scenery—and he and his dad had fallen out.

Over a woman.

"Keep your head down, and you might make partner someday," Ted said. "You have potential."

"Doing my best." Noah smiled weakly at Ted. Bottom line, Noah was great at his job—but he hated it. The only reason he'd gone into law was that his family expected it of him.

Goddamned family business.

He'd been groomed from a young age. It was a full family affair. Both his dad and mom were lawyers. Now his younger brother and him both. His brother loved it.

His sister had escaped deeply scathed.

She was an emotionally wounded dance instructor.

His brother, on the other hand, was the golden child. He had followed the path his parents had guided him down. Wife, family—big fucking house. They even had a little dog named Scout.

The woman who had sent Noah retreating from his family to another firm—Cynthia. She had been nice enough. Intelligent—funny. She was a legal assistant in his parents' firm. They'd been on a few dates together. Had some nice dinners. He'd even gritted his teeth through sex with her.

Then, she'd wanted more.

His family had wanted more.

Noah grunted and took a sip of his wine. He'd told his dad in no uncertain terms that he would never consider marrying her. No explanation was given. Just that he wasn't interested.

His decision hadn't sat well with anyone in his family. He was accused of being difficult. Why didn't he want to get married to a nice girl? Why didn't he want children?

Why didn't he want a full life?

Because the kind of life they wanted for him felt wrong—that's why. He'd decided to forge a new path when his dad wouldn't leave him alone about the *perfect match*.

Noah smiled at the server. He was a young guy probably in his 20s. Definitely gay. Way too young. Not something he typically cared about when he headed to The Marshes, a bird sanctuary on the edge of downtown. It had winding, secluded paths amongst the reeds and long grasses.

It came alive at night.

Maybe the guy's mouth had even been on his cock already.

He flitted his gaze from the guy's lips to his eyes.

He hated that part of his life.

"I'll have the lasagna," Noah said.

Ted finished his glass of wine. "Me too … and more wine."

Lunch passed with more discussion about client accounts they were individually working on. Ted gave Noah some pointers on his difficult ones. Answered some questions.

They arrived back in the office without a second to spare. His head was buzzing. He'd uncharacteristically had two glasses of wine. Noah's client would already be waiting for him. He dialed his assistant, Carol's, number. "Can you bring the client to the lakeside boardroom?"

"Sure thing. Be there in a second with him."

Noah gathered up his notebook and headed for the boardroom with the lake view. He used it whenever he had the chance. The view from his office just looked at a bunch of trees.

He waited near the door, ready to extend his hand in greeting.

His arm fell to his side as he watched who walked through the door.

Cole fucking Harrison.

"Oh," Cole whispered. "I ...um." He turned to Carol. "Can I reschedule with someone else?"

Carol furrowed her brow. "Noah is our best. He'll take good care of you."

Cole inhaled a long breath and crossed his arms as Carol left them. He scanned the room as if he were looking for another exit, then met Noah's gaze. He seemed resigned.

He nodded.

"Noah."

"Cole."

Immediately, Noah was back in high school, watching Cole, his once best friend, flirting with every boy who showed any interest. The ache in his heart returned, nearly dropping him.

Cole was even more beautiful now than he had been back then. The shaved head was a little shocking but it amplified his high cheekbones. His eyes were still starlit pools of emeralds.

His lips were still pouty and kissable.

But he looked tired.

The last time he had set his eyes on Cole had been during their high school prom. He'd nearly crumbled to his knees as Cole took off into the night with a guy he'd been dancing with all evening.

Time had aged Cole into something elegant. Like fine wine. Slim, long legs in pale pink linen pants. A sheer white, iridescent tank top hanging from his lean shoulders. Noah could just make out the dark outlines of Cole's nipples. Cole shifted from one high-heeled foot to the other.

Noah swallowed. "Have a seat." He motioned to a chair. "What can I help you with?"

"It's been a while." Cole pulled out a chair and sat across

the table from Noah.

Noah was slow but he took a seat. "Sixteen years."

"Is that going to be a problem … our history?"

Noah stared straight at Cole. He could do this. It might be the wine talking but he was willing to give it a go. Force the erupting feelings deep into his gut.

"Don't know why it should be."

Cole smirked. "So … you're a lawyer. Big surprise."

"I didn't have much of a choice in the matter." Noah flipped open his notebook and clicked his pen, ready to start writing. "What can I help you with?"

Cole lifted a large envelope onto the table. "My dad died three weeks ago."

Shit.

Noah had always liked Cole's dad. He was a down-to-earth, supportive man who remained in Cole's corner when Cole came out as gay. He'd stayed proud of his son.

"I'm sorry for your loss."

The number of times he'd said that. This time Noah meant it from his heart. Their long years of friendship came flooding back. At one time, Cole had been his best friend.

"Are you all right?" he asked Cole.

"I'm still in shock. It was a heart attack. Quick. One day, he was there. The next—gone."

"He was young."

"Still in his 50s."

"You here for help executing his will?"

"Eventually, but I wish it was that simple. My mom was named executor."

"Are you going to bring her in?"

Noah released a short, curt laugh. "No can do. Mom has dementia. She's in care."

"Jeezus, Cole. I'm sorry." Noah leaned forward and extended his hand. He was happy when Cole didn't take it. He wasn't sure what he would do with the sensation of touching Cole again.

"My life is a bit of a shitshow at the moment."

"So, what do you need from me … as a lawyer?"

"Two things. I'm the alternate power of attorney for my mom. Gotta fix that. Also, I'm the alternate executor of my dad's will. Need to become the primary or enact or somehow."

"Let's start with your mom. Are they letting you guide her care?"

"Sort of. They know she doesn't have anyone else in her corner at the moment. My sisters aren't picking up the ball at all. I'm all alone in this. The care home and health authority would prefer to have the official paperwork. That way I can sign documents … etcetera."

"Let's start there. It's an easy thing. I just need you to sign a statutory declaration. We'll need a doctor's letter stating your mom can't make legal decisions because of her dementia. Then you can take over as power of attorney for your mom because your dad passed away. We can do that by next week, then you can include the stat dec with any copies of the POA they need."

Cole sighed and relaxed. He leaned back in his chair.

"That's a weight lifted right there. I have so much paperwork sitting on my dining room table right now to have my dad's pensions transferred to Mom. I can't do that without the POA."

"Have you got the death certificate?"

"Yup." Cole opened the envelope on the table and pulled out the grey-green and beige certificate Noah had seen many times before. He had focused solely on helping people with the executorship of wills, including probate. He'd spent the past eight years doing it.

Noah looked at the paper. It seemed to be in order.

"Can I have a list of names either included in the will or those who might have interest in the will? We have to make sure there are no conflicts with our current clients."

"Sure, yeah." Cole rattled off a list. Noah jotted them down. He recognized most of them. Cole had two younger sisters. They'd been married over the years that had passed. There was no additional name associated with Cole. The fact made Noah's heart beat a little faster.

He cleared his throat.

The shield came up reminding him that he had hated Cole for years. Hated how Cole had come to terms with his sexuality without skipping a beat. Hated how easily Cole had come out as gay to his family. Hated how Cole had embraced his gayness and blossomed into a sexual being.

The two of them had practically grown up together. Met in kindergarten and became inseparable. Their lives had been completely intertwined. Until that night in junior year.

They were hunkered down in their sleeping bags at a sleepover at Cole's house.

"I think I'm gay," Cole had whispered to him.

Noah had laid there all night, staring at Cole asleep on the floor beside him. His love for Cole had been growing for years. Knowing Cole might be open to it made things worse. It was a secret he had intended to take to his grave. His family would never understand.

Or accept him as being gay.

It had been too painful to be around Cole after that.

Every chance Noah had, he ditched Cole or ignored him until Cole got the message. They weren't friends for long after that. It was the only way Noah knew to protect his heart.

The hatred had come over time. Cole was so comfortable with who he was, it was infuriating to Noah. Cole had moved on without him without even looking back—without saying a word. Deep down, he'd hoped Cole would put up a fight. But he had his queer friends to support him.

With every boy Cole latched onto, Noah put another cinder

block in the wall of hatred he had for Cole. Soon that wall was high enough that Noah couldn't see past it to what had once been an amazing friendship. It seemed the resentment was still there.

Cole was out and proud.

Noah was resigned to sneaking around in the shadows.

"Give me a few days and I'll draw up some paperwork for you to sign regarding your mom." Noah rose from his chair. "Then we can move onto your dad's estate."

Cole ascended from his chair like a fucking mythical unicorn, all smiles, and gorgeous lines. Cole extended his hand but Noah ignored it. He did not want to be plagued by the feel of Cole's hand in his. This was going to be difficult enough working with him.

Chapter Three | Cole

The dark beard and mustache looked good on him, Noah. Didn't wipe out the fact his best friend had abandoned him when he told him he thought he might be gay. He had expected Noah to be shocked by his admission, but not to dump him on the side of the road like a bag of garbage.

Noah had been complete in his rejection. And he'd been cruel. Ignoring Cole in the hallways, not answering his calls, walking away when Cole started talking to him, and joining in when other boys ridiculed him. Cole still harbored sadness and a lot of hatred toward Noah over it.

When he was told he'd be seeing a Noah, he never imagined it would be his Noah. His Noah, if he became a lawyer, would work for the family law firm.

What the hell was he doing somewhere else?

Didn't matter. Cole was going to phone the law firm and ask to be assigned to someone else. He did not need to see Noah ever again if he had a choice.

Cole jiggled open his mailbox. Mostly flyers. Three letters. Two to do with his dad's estate. One he knew would fix a lot of problems. He ripped it open. A check for two thousand dollars.

An easy two thousand dollars, too. All he had to do was have his drag persona, Trixie Lamour, entertain a wedding party. Tell wild stories about the brides. Embarrass the family members and weddinggoers at large. Be a general nuisance of a clown. It was going to be a blast.

Plus, free accommodation for the weekend.

Free food.

And an open bar.

He just needed to get there. His compact SUV was on its last legs. Driving all the way to Kaslo, BC in the Kootenays was going to take some praying.

He remembered Naomi and Debbie from high school. He had never pegged either of them as gay but sometime in the last couple of years, they had bumped into each other—and stuck.

Cole folded the check and tucked it in the front pocket of his small, white sequined, over-shoulder bag. He'd take a picture of the check upstairs and deposit it.

Tonight, he had another show. He rarely took a break. It was Amateur Night at the bar. He was hosting, giving new drag performers on the scene an opportunity to perform.

It would be a slow Tuesday night, but it was money to line his pocket.

In his apartment, he shoved aside some hats and slumped onto his sofa. Noah was bouncing around in Cole's mind. The man was nice to look at. Too bad he was a homophobe.

He leaned forward and placed his forehead in his palms. Sweat gathered along his spine. Noah hadn't filled his mind in years. There had been a time when Noah occupied his every thought.

God, if things had been different between us.

He had prayed for things to be different between them.

Noah had walked away before he'd been able to talk to him about his growing feelings.

Water under the bridge.

Cole whipped out the check, found an empty spot on the sofa arm, opened his banking app, took a picture, and deposited the money into his account.

The influx bumped his balance up to fourteen hundred and sixty.

He'd been deep in his overdraft.

Feeling a tiny bit of relief, Cole wandered into the kitchen. In the freezer, he had some premade, heatable meals. He chose a sweet-and-sour chicken bowl and tossed it in the microwave.

He took a seat at his dining room table to wait.

Damned Noah again.

Cole pinched the bridge of his nose. Those amber eyes had looked at him with such sympathy and kindness. Then they'd shifted and become cold.

Noah still hated him.

He still hated Noah.

The microwave beeped. Tomorrow he'd phone the law firm. Tell them he was taking his business elsewhere. That would be the end of that. He and Noah had managed to avoid each other for sixteen years. They could easily do it for another sixteen. Hopefully more.

He ate his food and then painted his face in modest drag. There was no need to go full out. Even with what would classify as a women's night out makeup, he was still Trixie.

Trixie light.

Not wanting to completely tuck, Cole chose a long, flowing chiffon, aquamarine dress. A simple gaff would do the trick to conceal his man bits.

He decided to catch a cab, not wanting to drive. He needed to give his car plenty of rest before their big trek on Friday. The week would hopefully fly by fast. Tomorrow was Drag Bingo. Then Thursday was Drag Karaoke. Friday was the welcome night of the wedding celebrations. It would take Cole five hours to reach the resort and then he'd have two hours to get ready.

He still wasn't sure what costumes he was going to take. Some newer ones might be a good idea. People would want to have pictures taken with him. Most of his older costumes smelled like the inside of an old gym shoe. He wouldn't want to stand too close to anyone in those.

He paid the cabbie and hauled open the door to the bar. It was like a second home in there. A few tables of people were chatting, attempting to be heard over the loud music.

Cole wandered up to the bar and pursed his lips. The sultry Miguel was working behind it, polishing glasses and pouring drinks. His black t-shirt hugged his pecs and showed off his smooth, contracting, hard-at-work biceps. Cole leaned against the bar top.

He'd wanted to sleep with Miguel for weeks.

Apparently, he had a boyfriend who refused to share him.

Cole tapped the bar top. "Could I get a bottle of Okanagan Hills pinot gris?"

"Two glasses with it or one?"

Cole looked around. "Only seeing one of me today."

"Unlike Saturday night. Pretty sure there were three of you. And all of them were all over me." Miguel smirked. "Not that I'm complaining."

"I can be a bit handsy."

Miguel leaned forward and lowered his voice. "You nearly gave me a handjob in the bathroom. Frances would have killed me if you had managed to get your hand down my pants."

Cole stepped back. He couldn't remember anything like that happening. He grabbed his bottle of wine and the wine glass and found a vacant table to sit at.

A handjob?

Miguel?

It honestly wasn't clicking. He sat up straight and pretended to be busy on his phone. Inside, he was dying. It was getting bad. He knew it was getting bad, the drinking. He'd been nearly off the rails for a long time, but off the rails enough to drive his husband away.

Darren hadn't deserved that—what he'd put him through.

Darren had been patient with him.

But even he'd been stretched beyond what he could endure. The word *trainwreck* had been used.

Cole poured himself his first glass. He was two glasses in when it was time for him to start the show. He looked into the third glass he had poured. Something in him didn't want it. He knew he could do this show with his eyes closed. He wasn't sure he even needed the alcohol.

Perhaps, he could set it aside for one night.

Let Trixie out to play without being drunk.

Was that even possible?

Trixie's persona *was* alcohol-fueled. He'd only ever played her that way. Cole pushed the wine glass aside. He was going to try. He owed his dad that much. The week before he died, his dad had opened a conversation with him about his drinking. Cole had promised to try to stop.

Cole rose from his seat, jumped on stage, and grabbed a microphone.

"All right, all you bitches! Who's ready to cheer on some baby drag monsters!"

The drive was more pleasant than Cole had been expecting. He'd never ventured into the Kootenays before. With each turn, the forest became greener, and the mountains vaulted higher. More mystical at every bend. He felt like he was winding his way into an enchanted realm.

And his car was holding out. Full of gas on departure. Not overheating. No scary engine lights. And no tires threatening to burst. The last one was a gamble. He needed new tires.

He rumbled across a bridge and into town. He'd passed the entrance to the resort on purpose. He wanted to check out the *downtown* area of Kaslo. The view out his passenger window behind a pioneer day hotel caught his eye. He drove down a street closer to the lake and parked the car.

He wandered over to the edge of the embankment.

Oh, wow!

He'd never seen anything like it. Kootenay Lake. The water was still, clear, and blue, and the evergreen-covered mountains angled up sharply away from it. He'd read that in the early spring, the mountain tops remained snowcapped for weeks, reflected on the glass-like water.

He turned around and took a closer look at the hotel he had circled in behind. It was aptly named Kaslo Hotel and had easily been built in the late 1800s when Kaslo was a silver ore town. The building was burgundy with cream trim, three stories. It reminded Cole of buildings you might see in old Western movies. Cole called up the town's history on his phone.

Kaslo had been wiped out in a flood in 1894 but rebuilt. Impressive. There used to be more people living there. Around three thousand but then the silver rush faded and people drifted away. The economy was saved by the introduction of fruit farming and logging. It was also the site of a Japanese internment camp in 1942, a time in history to be ashamed of in Canada.

Cole turned back to face the water and took a picture, then spun around and took a selfie with the lake and mountains in the background. He'd probably never see the place again.

Back in his car, Cole drove back along the road to the resort. It was nestled amongst towering evergreen trees and had a view of the lake. It was smaller than Cole had expected it to be. Debbie had told him some people were staying at the Kaslo Hotel. Only her favorite people were staying at the resort where the festivities would be happening. It seemed performers got priority as well.

He hauled the first of his luggage from the back of his vehicle and rolled it across the gravel parking lot. There were two more massive bags and a makeup case still in his car. It was a wonder he had fit everything into the back. He'd had to put the back seats down.

He bumped the first bag up the steep steps and left it in front of the entrance doors. Luckily, a cute male guest came out and offered to help him with the rest of his bags. Together, they managed to get all three suitcases and the makeup case into the lobby area.

The guy promised to seek him out later.

Cole did a slow turnaround, looking at the space. It screamed log cabin … but on an epic scale. Warm wood, light streaming in the windows, the slight smell of cedar from the boughs someone had brought in and decorated with. It was very relaxing.

"You're in room 201." A bubbly young woman handed him a keycard. "One of the brides asked me to inform you that you'll be sharing with another guest."

Cole frowned. His costumes and other crap were going to take up much of the room. Why on earth had Debbie thought it was a good idea for him to share a room with someone?

"Who with?" he asked.

"I'm not supposed to say."

Well, that was helpful. A surprise roommate. Hopefully, Debbie hadn't paired him with someone who used to bully him in high school. That would be a nightmare.

For whom, he wasn't sure.

"Thank you." Cole took the keycard. He looked around for the elevator. "Elevator?"

"Sorry, no, just stairs."

"Can someone help me? I've got a lot of heavy stuff."

"Sure thing." The young woman lifted the phone and asked someone for some assistance for a guest. They were quick to show up. A very sexy guy in his mid-30s grasped the handles of two of Cole's rolling bags and started up the stairs. Cole watched the guy's ass as he ascended.

Sweet.

He'd like to take a bite out of that.

Wonder if he's gay.

Cole refocused and followed the guy up the stairs and down a short hallway to room 201. He thanked him. Gave him a wink … just in case. But the guy grunted and turned away.

That would be a no.

He used his keycard, opened the door, and entered the room. It was standard as far as hotel rooms went. Two double beds, a desk, bedside tables, and a dresser with a television on top.

Cole checked the closet space. It had enough width for him to pack his costumes into. He started with those, pulling them from two of his bags and hanging them on hangers he had brought from home. You never knew with hotels. You didn't want to end up with no hangers.

Next were his wigs. He had only brought three. He lay them flat on the dresser, crowding the top of it entirely along with his jewelry; three rhinestone and crystal necklaces with matching earrings, lots of sparkly bangles, and a tiara for good measure.

He turned to the desk and positioned his strip-lit makeup mirror, plugged it in, then opened his makeup case and began setting out all the tools of his glamorous trade.

He snorted out a laugh.

Glamorous, my ass.

He only had one and a half hours to get ready. His detour into town had put him behind schedule. But it had been worth it. The scenery here was stunning.

He dumped all his tucking supplies in the bathroom, littering the countertop, along with his glue spray and hairdryer. His razor, toothbrush, and toothpaste filled the remaining space.

Whomever his roommate was, he hoped they didn't have

much stuff.

Cole sat down at the desk. It was going to be a long night. He needed to beat his face hard and thick to withstand the passage of time. He got to work.

Just as he finished his lips, the door of the room opened and a man walked in.

He caught the man's face in his mirror.

Oh, for fuck's sake.

Chapter Four | Noah

It took Noah a second to process what and whom he was looking at. The person in his room was sitting at the desk, bare legs—shirtless. He promptly verified it was a guy. He was bald and his face was done up in makeup that made him look like an overly dramatized woman.

Noah looked around the room. His drag crap was everywhere.

The man looked over his shoulder at him. High cheekbones, delicate jaw … emerald green eyes. Noah dropped one of his bags to the floor.

Oh, for fuck's sake.

It was Cole.

Cole was a fucking drag queen.

Noah's stomach sank. This couldn't be happening. When Noah arrived at the front desk and was told he would be sharing his room with another guest, he'd been annoyed. Debbie hadn't told him he'd have to endure a roommate for the weekend.

Now, to find out it was Cole.

A drag queen Cole.

He lifted his phone from his pocket and texted her.

Noah: <What the hell?!>

Debbie: <You don't like your surprise?>

Noah: <What were you thinking?>

Debbie: <That you two were best friends all through school.>

Noah: <Not at the end we weren't.>

Debbie: <I thought it would give you a chance to reconcile.>

Noah: <Why?>
Debbie: <Because you were such good friends once.>
Noah: <Find me a different room.>
Debbie: <There isn't one. Suck it up.>
Noah grunted and scanned the room.
Noah: <His drag crap is everywhere.>
Debbie: <It'll be entertaining. You need to learn to loosen up.>
Noah stuffed his phone back in his pocket.
Loosen up.
Bah.
"Were you texting Debbie?" Cole asked.
"Yeah. She says we're stuck with each other."
"Did she do it on purpose?"
"Looks that way."
Cole sighed and turned back to his mirror. "I'll be in here a lot getting ready, changing costumes and such. You might want to get acquainted with a lounge of some sort."
"There's one off the front entry." Noah had spotted it on the way in. It didn't look to have coffee but there were leather sofas to relax in and gaze out at the view of the lake. He'd be spending a lot of time down there. He looked around again. "Where am I supposed to put my stuff?"
"The drawers are mostly empty."
"And my suit?"
Cole twisted around to look at Noah.
"Back of the bathroom door?"
Noah grunted as he threw his bags on one bed. He unzipped the garment bag and checked his suit, then took the bag into the bathroom and hung it on the back of the door.
His attention fell on the bathroom counter. He lifted a roll of gauze and a bag full of what looked like thin beige menstrual pads.
What the fuck?

He tossed them back on the counter.

"Don't touch my stuff," Cole hollered from the bedroom.

"Wasn't planning on it."

When he re-entered the bedroom, Cole was standing near the closet, flipping through the ridiculous clothes he had brought with him. He was wearing a pink G-string and nothing else.

Noah's face flushed and he looked away.

Cole's body had never looked like that when they were friends. They'd swum and changed in front of each other all their lives ... until that night. Now, Cole had lean lines, muscled forearms and thighs, and abs that were cut and smooth. Not a hair in sight anywhere on his body.

And his bare ass ... oh, my god, his ass.

Firm globes of lickable flesh poised high above his thighs.

Noah's cock stirred.

"I'm going downstairs," he announced, needing to get as far away from Cole as he could.

"Welcome party dinner is in forty-five minutes. There's a banquet hall around back."

"You'll be there, I suppose."

Cole smiled at him. Not an earnest smile. A smile that bordered on sardonic.

"With Trixie Lamour bells on."

Noah huffed out of the room and slammed the door. He'd put the rest of his clothes in the drawers later. He wouldn't be staying long at the welcome party. Not with Cole there doing god knows what. Performing? Bantering with guests? He knew what drag routines entailed. He'd never been to one but he knew how boorish they could become. He wanted no part of it.

Loosen up.

Shut it, Debbie.

He slung himself into a leather sofa near a window in the lounge. It shouldn't have come as a surprise that Cole was a drag queen. After coming out, Cole had been so comfortable with his sexuality. He'd started to dress differently—more feminine. He'd emphasized his flamboyant mannerisms that Noah had always assumed were little quirks. Like Cole was just dramatic.

Cole had been all out gay in school.

From deep within his own closet, Noah had hated Cole for it.

Now, he had to share a room with him. Potentially unearth the feelings he once had for Cole. How badly it had hurt to see Cole thrive. How badly it had hurt to want him so desperately.

He held his breath, then exhaled.

Maybe he should go home.

Or to another hotel. He pulled out his phone. There were a couple of other places to stay in town. He phoned them all. Every one of them was booked solid.

"Hey!" Debbie appeared beside him. She leaned down and kissed Noah's cheek. "So glad you came, Noah. Senior year was epic with you."

Noah laughed. "You used to call me an asshole a lot."

"That's just because I had a crush on you." Debbie sat on the arm of the sofa and flung her arm around Noah's shoulders. "Naomi obliterated all attraction I had toward men."

"Were you and her a thing in high school?"

Debbie clicked her tongue. "I never kiss and tell."

Noah laughed and looked up at her. "Oh, my god … you were."

"Not telling." She walked her fingers down Noah's arm. "Speaking of which, how are you and Cole getting along?"

Noah sat forward in his seat. "Cole and I never had a thing."

"Could have fooled me the way your eyes used to follow him everywhere."

"You're delusional." Noah rose to his feet. "Is that why you put us together? To try and rekindle something that never existed between us in the first place?"

"You used to be best friends. I never totally understood what happened between you. You were pretty harsh on him when he came out. Abandoned him. Even hung out with his bullies."

"And you didn't think it might be a good idea to just leave that alone?"

Debbie crossed her arms. "You don't have any regrets about the way you treated him?"

Noah heaved out an exaggerated sigh. "Fuck … of course, I do."

"Then fix it. You have all weekend."

"You're meddling."

"Look …." Debbie took a step toward him. "Naomi and I fell out during the first year of university. It was eight years later that we ran into each other. What we had fought about that dissolved our friendship wasn't important anymore. Here and now … we love each other."

"Our relationship was different. Cole and I were just friends."

"Then mend the friendship."

Noah looked out the window and thought about it for a second. The hatred was still there, burning just below the surface. Cole had been enjoying a life Noah could only dream about. His best friend had moved on without him. He'd been left standing on a pier without his boat.

He'd screamed and thrashed and destroyed his room the morning after Cole told him he thought he might be gay. His poor heart had been in agony as though it was being stomped on.

For Cole to be so close—but untouchable.

It had nearly broken him.

They'd never been in the same space alone together again. He made sure of it. He stopped answering Cole's phone calls.

Wouldn't open the door if he saw it was him. He carried around mountains of books from class to class so he could avoid going to their shared locker.

He had wiped the guy from his life.

Now, Cole would be in his face for two nights in a row.

"I really wish you hadn't tried to force my hand," he said.

"I'm sorry." Debbie reached forward and touched Noah's face. "Try to make the best of it."

"I'll try ... but you haven't heard the end of me complaining about it." Noah started to add something else but a loud voice rang out from the front entry staircase, drowning him out.

"Let's get this party started, bitches!"

It could only be one person. Cole had emerged as Trixie and was sweeping down the stairs, laughing and cajoling, and reading people for filth as he passed by them.

"Follow me, everyone!" Trixie marched past the entrance to the lounge, then took a step back and peered in at Noah. "You too mister surly and sexy. Surely, you don't want to miss out on all this." She smoothed her hands down the front of her dress from tits to hips and pursed her lips at Noah. "I'm not leaving this building without you riding my ass to the banquet hall."

Noah rolled his eyes.

And it begins.

Not wanting to suffer any more of Trixie's attention, Noah followed along behind the other people making their way outside and around the back of the building. They approached a barn-like structure lit up with strings of tiny white lights. Come nightfall, it would look magical.

Inside were rows and rows of rustic picnic benches, some stretching fifteen feet long at least on their own. There were white linen table runners each with intermittent eruptions of local flowers is old metal milk jugs. Each cutlery setting was sparkling, reflecting the twinkle lights hanging from the rafters. Noah looked up at the loft area. He almost expected to see hay up there.

The effect of the decorations was mesmerizing. Debbie and Naomi had chosen well. It was the kind of place he would like to get married in someday.

He stuffed his hands in his pockets.

Marriage. It was a dream.

A dream he preferred to keep buried.

After finding his name in calligraphy by a place setting, Noah climbed over the bench seating and tried to get comfortable on the hard, rough wood. He looked to either side at the names of the place settings beside him. Cole's name wasn't there.

He almost felt disappointed.

Almost.

And then Trixie started speaking.

She was obviously the emcee for the welcome party and dinner. And from the onset, it looked like things were going to get raunchy. The crowd seemed all right with that. They were already laughing and clapping at Trixie's insanely debauched language.

Noah examined the crowd. No one less than forty. Mixed—straight and gay. They'd hired Trixie for a reason. They were looking for a fun, crude weekend.

He watched Trixie move back and forth across the top of the space, then down each aisle. He couldn't believe it was Cole up there. So self-assured. So confident. So brash. This persona was strutting around with more performance prowess than Noah thought Cole was capable of.

Cole had always been a little outgoing on the outside.

But inside … inside, Cole was a shy, sensitive, scared, sweet …."

Noah played with his fork, flipping it over and over.

"Straight couples!" Trixie shouted. "Straight men … cover

your eyes." She paced through the crowd, encouraging some of the men to cover their eyes. "Okay. This is a scientific study."

She smiled at the crowd. Most men had their eyes covered.

"Women ... show of hands if you like to take it up the ass."

Noah groaned and covered his face. The room burst out laughing.

He lowered his hand and looked around the space. Some women were timidly holding up their hands. Others were practically leaping out of their seats.

"Interesting ... interesting." Trixie nodded as she walked. "Now women, hands down, cover your eyes. Straight men ... at ease. You can look again." She struck a sexy pose as the men lowered their hands and laughed as a few men whistled at her. "Okay, now this is the really important part of the study. All you men—straight men only, raise your hand if you want to give it in the ass."

Lots of men laughed and lots of hands went up. Trixie pretended to be counting them. "All right ... all right." She waved the men's hands down. "Lower your hands. Women open your eyes. The men have voted and we seem to have a problem."

This statement brought on a round of laughter. Everyone knew where Trixie was going with this. She said it anyway. "It seems that more men put up their hands than women."

"What does that mean?" someone shouted.

Trixie pointed her finger at random people, sweeping the crowd.

"It means some of you straight couples need to have a serious conversation tonight. Or perhaps some of these men need to talk to the gay men in the room. And arrange a date."

The room erupted in applause.

God's sake.

Noah glanced around. When were they going to start

serving food? He didn't know if he could take any more of this. His innocent Cole had turned into something unrecognizable.

Apparently, the banter was just a warm-up. Loud music burst through speakers Noah hadn't even noticed. Trixie took center stage at the front of the room.

The song came to the vocal bit and Trixie started lip syncing as she strolled and gyrated to the music. She messed up the hair of a few men and leaned in against them, then danced her back down one blushing guy until she was squatting. She popped back up and headed straight for Noah.

A full-on beeline toward him.

Noah was horrified when Trixie slung her boot over his shoulder and pressed her sequined groin against his back. She threaded her fingers through his hair. Her big fake breasts pressed against the back of his head, messing up his hair. She ground against him for an entire chorus.

Then her foot was gone and she was off dancing down the aisle to harass her next victim. She gave other men and some women the same treatment.

Noah convinced himself that he was simply a casualty.

A targeted one.

When the song was over, Trixie kept a smile on her face as she approached the bar. Noah watched her smile fade when she placed an order. Uncertainty flitted across her face as she stared at the bar top, waiting. A bottle of wine. One glass. Every time someone approached her, Trixie's face would light up and she'd become animated. Then as soon as the fan moved away, the bright eyes and smile would recede to reveal the shy, scared best friend he'd grown up with.

Cole.

Not Trixie—Cole.

Cole lifted the bottle and glass, turned, and headed for a back room.

Noah had the urge to follow him.

"All right, everyone. Food is ready."

A hoot of excitement went up. Noah stared at where Cole had gone.

He's a big boy.

He'll be fine.

The food was delicious. An assortment of hot meats and fresh salads. Fruit and dessert. Noah hadn't realized how hungry he was. He checked the banquet table for the tenth time. He hadn't seen Cole approach to dish himself up some food. Again, Noah felt like going to look for him.

"Everyone get themselves stuffed and satisfied!"

Trixie was back. And she was all the way *on*. It made Noah nervous to watch her. There was more than one bottle of wine in her. No one else seemed to notice. Or if they did, they didn't care. Shots of clear liquid started showing up on the table in front of Trixie.

"Balls up!" Trixie threw back the first of many shots.

After the fifth one, Noah couldn't watch anymore. He excused himself from the people he hadn't even made an effort to speak to on either side of him.

His attention had been solely on Cole.

His once best friend was back to occupying his every thought.

The keycard didn't work on the first try and for a second, Noah thought he might have the wrong room, but then he walked into the chaos created by his roommate.

This was the right room.

Noah closed the door behind him. He was exhausted. The long drive. The big meal. And the unveiling of Trixie Lamour, Cole's alter-ego. He sat on the bed and surveyed the room.

He wasn't going to worry about the mess.

He stripped off his shirt over his head and made for the

bathroom. He was brushing his teeth when the door to their room burst open and smashed into the wall.

"Noah!"

The bathroom door flew open and Cole collapsed against it as though it was the only thing holding him up. A wine glass in one hand—a full open bottle in the other.

"Oh, you … are here," Cole slurred. "I couldn't see you … anywhere."

Noah spat, rinsed his mouth, and turned to Cole, one hand on his hip. "I was tired."

"I have … the solution for that." Cole lifted the glass of red wine, sloshing some onto the bathroom floor. "Have a little sip." He held it out for Noah to take.

Cole was barely standing.

Noah raised a hand. "No. Thanks. I'm going to bed." He pushed past Cole, almost knocking him over, and pulled back the covers of a bed. He sat on the edge and hauled off his jeans.

"You're no fun." Cole pouted at Noah and stumbled into the room. "You were … never any fun. You could always … suck the breath … out of the fun … in the room."

Cole tripped closer.

"Right. That's why we were friends for so long." Noah burrowed under the covers and pulled the blankets over his shoulder as he rolled onto his side. Deliberately not facing Cole.

The air conditioning blasted in the room.

"You had … your moments." Cole plopped down on the corner of Noah's bed.

"Goodnight, Cole."

"Hold up … I have things … I want to say to you."

Noah could see out of the corner of his eye that Cole was accentuating each word with the movement of his hands. Including the hand gripping the wine glass.

A small amount of wine splashed onto his blankets.

You've got to be kidding me.

"Go back to the party," Noah said.

"Not until I've said ... said ... what I want to say."

Noah rolled onto his back. "And what would that be?" Before he had a chance to defend himself, Cole rose to his feet, held the full bottle of wine over Noah's head, and poured.

"That you're ... an asshole."

Noah jerked upright, wiping the wine from his face, sputtering and coughing. His face, his hair, his chest—his pillow and blankets were drenched in pungent liquid.

"Jeezus fuck! You're fucking insane!"

"No." Cole pointed at him. "What's insane is that you ... you ... ditched me ... you fucking homophobe. A lifetime of friendship." He simulated an explosion with his fingers. "Poof."

"You're crazy." Noah leaped out of bed. He needed to wash the wine out of his hair and off his skin. He stalked into the bathroom and turned on the water in the shower.

He could hear Cole clunking around in the room. He hoped Cole would leave and find somewhere else to sleep. Surely, with the number of gay men at the welcome party, there had to be one willing to take Trixie Lamour on for the night.

Noah took his time, wanting the room to be empty when he emerged from the bathroom. His clean underwear was in his luggage in the middle of the room.

He was out of luck.

Cole sat at the desk using some kind of wipes to clean the makeup off his face. His wig was discarded on the dresser. Shoes in the middle of the floor. Costume draped across the bed.

The clean bed.

Noah looked at the bed he'd been lying in. It was soaked like a bloody murder scene of red. The mattress was likely ruined.

Great.

An expensive unwelcome charge was going to hit his credit card.

He crossed the room, lifted the costume, and hung it over the television. Cole was tracking him in his little mirror. Noah pulled back the covers of the clean bed and climbed in.

Fuck underwear.

Cole spun in his chair, his arm hanging over the back of it.

"Where am I ... supposed to sleep?"

"You should have thought about that before you dumped wine on me."

Cole harrumphed. "You ... deserved it."

"Sleep in the tub. I'm sure there are extra blankets and pillows in the closet." Noah lifted his head and stared at Cole. "Or the floor. I don't really care."

"You never ... cared." Cole threw his last wipe of the night into the garbage.

Noah sat up. "What's that supposed to mean?"

"If you cared ... why did you ... hate me?"

Noah could feel his pulse increase. The hate—that was something he wasn't going to explain to Cole. How he'd fallen in love with his best friend—but couldn't have him.

How he couldn't even tell him he loved him.

How he couldn't tell Cole how it had broken his heart every time he saw Cole with another guy. How the animosity had built in him.

So, he lied.

"I never hated you."

"Jeezus ... Noah. You're such a ... fucking ... liar." Cole nearly fell off the chair as he removed himself from it. He tripped and landed on his ass on the bed near Noah's feet.

Cole placed his hand on Noah's ankle. The grip was light and comfortable. Noah had vivid memories of Cole doing the same thing when they were kids.

He did it when he needed assurance.

"You have … no idea," Cole said. "What you … put me through."

"I never meant to hurt you."

Cole whipped his hand away. "Yes, you did." He leaped to his feet. "I have to piss."

Noah furrowed his brow as Cole crossed the room. There was a small strip of beige material across Cole's lower back at the top of his ass crack. The lights in the bathroom flicked on.

When he returned, Cole was wearing the G-string; balls and cock visible beneath the thin pink material. Cole walked to the head of the bed and pressed his thighs to the mattress.

He wasn't wearing a shirt. His nipples were dark pink and hard as nubs.

Cole pushed Noah's shoulder. "Move over."

For fuck's sake.

"Fine."

Noah couldn't in good conscience let Cole sleep in the tub or on the floor. He shuffled over and made room for Cole in the bed. He rolled over so he was facing away from him.

Cole stunk of alcohol.

And he didn't want to be looking at him.

He sucked in a breath as Cole's back came in contact with his. Skin to skin. Back to back. Ass to ass, they had a brief moment of organizing their feet. Cole's feet were freezing.

Noah rolled his eyes as Cole placed his cold feet against Noah's warm calves.

Some things hadn't changed.

Flickering sunlight danced across the bed, waking him. Noah opened his eyes and sighed. Cole was plastered to his chest. His cheek on Noah's pec. An arm draped over Noah's belly.

Noah groaned in annoyance. His cock was as hard as the

rocky cliffs across the lake. Cole's proximity was making it worse. Every breath of Cole's was waking his cock even more.

Cole grumbled and shifted.

Not helping.

"I'm done with that," Cole mumbled softly then swatted at something imaginary. His hand came to rest on Noah's chest. He shook his head. "No," he whispered.

Noah closed his eyes. It was obvious Cole was still asleep. As a kid, the entire time Noah was in his life, Cole had suffered from nightmares, his daily fears plaguing him.

He set his hand on Cole's shoulder. His skin was cool. Always so cool. Noah lifted the blanket and covered Cole right up to his ear. Cole's hand closed then flexed on his chest.

"Oh." Cole popped his head up. "Oh … I'm so sorry." He flung the blanket off and scrambled out of bed. He fell on the floor in his haste, landing on his G-stringed ass.

"It's all right." Noah rolled to face Cole. He smiled at him. "You were entertaining me."

Cole's eyes grew wide. "We didn't …." He swallowed hard and pointed at the bed. He struggled to his feet. "Please tell me we didn't fuck."

Noah laughed. "What if we had?"

Cole sat on the other bed. "Then you'd have a lot of fucking explaining to do."

"Because you were drunk?"

"No." Cole ran his hand across the top of his head and closed his eyes. He looked as though he was about to throw up. He was suffering. "Because you're not gay, asshole."

Noah grinned wider. He was having fun with this. A bit of torment was just what Cole needed to increase his hangover. "Who said I'm not gay?"

Cole frowned at him. "You did."

Noah shook his head. "Never did."

"But you're not."

Noah bounded out of bed and headed for the bathroom. He was very aware of the fact his bare semi-hard cock cruised right past Cole's face. "*You* will never know."

"Noah!" Cole rushed the bathroom door as Noah closed it in his face.

"Sorry, can't hear you. Busy." Noah hovered over the toilet and emptied his bladder. He was going to take his time, knowing that Cole probably needed to puke.

Cole pounded on the door. "Tell me you're not gay!"

"What if that's not the truth!"

"Jeezus, Noah … I'm not playing! Tell me! Say it!"

Noah flushed and opened the door. "I'm not gay. Satisfied."

"Thank God." Cole pushed past Noah and into the bathroom, shoved him out, and shut the door. "You almost gave me a fucking heart attack!"

Noah leaned against the door. "Maybe I'm lying!"

"Asshole!" Then the sound of vomiting.

Noah chuckled as he walked away from the door. Cole had always been easy to harass. He dug around in his baggage and found some clothes that would be suitable for breakfast. There was a small dining room in the resort. He'd bring up a plate of dry toast for Cole.

Chapter Five | Cole

Cole stretched out on the bed and closed his eyes to stop the room from spinning. He rolled and pressed his face to the pillow Noah had been using. He could smell Noah's cologne on it.

He gathered up the pillow and snuggled it against his nose and lips.

Waking up like that, draped over Noah's chest would have been a dream if he hadn't been so horrified by his behavior. For half a second, he'd really thought they'd had sex.

He's not gay.

And he hates you.

Cole hummed against the pillow. But goddamn, he smelled good. And they'd fit together like they were meant to be. In an alternate universe, they would probably be together.

He licked his dry lips. He needed water.

He clambered off the bed and headed for the bathroom. One more round with his head in the toilet then he brushed his teeth and filled a glass with cold water. He downed the whole thing.

The door to the room opened.

He groaned. He'd wanted to be alone for the next couple of hours. He wasn't due to perform until this afternoon. The elite resort group was going for a nature walk two hours before the wedding ceremony and he was expected to accompany them fitted out in drag.

In heels.

Noah's face appeared at the edge of the bathroom doorway. "How are you feeling?"

"Rough." Cole coughed and left the bathroom. He might still have another few appointments with the porcelain bowl.

Right now, he needed to lie back down.

"I brought you toast."

Cole looked at Noah's outstretched hand. On it was a plate with a stack of dry white toast. His heart softened. This was the guy who supposedly hated him. His emotions were all over the place after waking up on him. The gesture was so stupid and confusingly sweet that he nearly cried.

He took the plate instead. "Thank you." He sat on the bed with his back against the headboard. It was a good idea to eat. He hadn't partaken of dinner last night. He was starving.

Cole munched the center bits out of two pieces of toast and then set the plate on the bedside table. He took a deep breath. He felt moderately better.

The whole time he was eating, Noah had sat on the chair by the desk and watched him.

"Better?" Noah asked.

"Gives me something to throw up later."

Noah frowned. "That wasn't the anticipated outcome. I noticed you didn't eat last night."

Why had Noah noticed that? Sure, everyone's eyes had been on Trixie, but surely Noah had been eating—not watching the banquet table. Maybe talking to his neighbors.

"Too busy drinking," Cole admitted.

"Noticed that too. Do you always drink like that?"

Loaded question. Most of the time? Was that an answer?

"I'm going through a lot of shit."

"Your dad?"

Cole shuffled down in the bed, pulled the covers up, and hugged Noah's pillow to him. He met Noah's gaze. It was still so easy to open up to him. "I haven't cried yet."

It was the truth. He'd been so shocked that he hadn't processed that his dad was gone. He kept expecting his phone to ring and he'd hear his dad's voice relaying a story.

He imagined dropping in at his childhood home and his dad

would be there.

He closed his eyes as tears welled up.

"I don't have a family home anymore. Christmas, holidays, birthday parties. We always gathered at my parents' house. Dad's gone. Mom's in care. The house is empty."

Noah sat on the edge of the bed and reached for Cole's hand.

Cole decided to let him have it. It was warm and comforting. It was what he needed to finally feel something and break down. The tears and surges of sobs rushed out from deep in his soul.

He looked up at Noah. "I'll never be able to go home again. It's gone."

"Jeezus, Cole." He stroked Cole's cheek. "Move over."

Noah lay on top of the blankets and covered Cole's chest with his arm. Noah's hand came to rest on Cole's shoulder. His thumb stroked it through the bedding.

Noah set his head down on the other half of Cole's pillow.

He could feel Noah's soft breath on the side of his neck.

I can never go home again.

The reality hit him.

Anguish swelled in him and more tears ran down his face, soaking the pillow. The noises he made for the next twenty minutes were part wailing—part hiccupping and gasping.

Noah held him through the whole thing.

It was a full-on breakdown.

"You're all right," Noah whispered against his skin. "You're strong. You can do this."

"I don't feel strong. I feel as if I'm falling apart."

"I believe in you."

Cole stiffened, shuddered, and gripped Noah's arm as Noah kissed the side of his face. Soft, tender lips. His heart raced to an unhealthy rate and almost beat out of his chest.

"I'm here for you," Noah whispered and nuzzled behind his

ear.

Cole snapped out of his grief.

What the hell was that?

"Noah?"

Noah snuggled closer to him. "Don't make me say it."

Cole blinked furiously as he stared up at the ceiling.

Say what?

He turned onto his shoulder to look at Noah. Noah angled back a little.

Their eyes met.

Noah made the first move. He cupped Cole's face, breathed across his lips, tentative—slow, watching the movement of Cole's eyes, then sealed their lips together.

Cole hesitated at first, filled with disbelief.

Why now?

He released his question to the universe.

He would deal with it later.

The kiss felt good. So right—so pure—so destined. He kissed Noah back, testing the connection. A fire ignited in him, setting his body ablaze. He gripped Noah's head and deepened the kiss. Years of craving Noah's lips overtook every stop sign flashing in his mind.

Keeping contact with Cole's lips, Noah hauled the blanket off Cole's shoulders. He brushed his fingers up and down Cole's bare arm, then across his collarbone.

Reality and Cole's sensibilities rushed in.

He placed his hand on Noah's chest and pushed him away.

"What are we doing?"

Noah studied Cole's eyes. "I'm fulfilling something I've wanted to do for a long time."

A wave of anxiety rose in Cole's chest. This was going to end badly. He wanted it. He wanted that closeness. He'd craved it for years. But this was something that shouldn't be rushed.

"You're gay?" Cole asked.

Noah chewed on his bottom lip. "Pretty sure."

Cole's eyebrows shot up. "You haven't tested the theory?"

"Once." Noah looked down at Cole's chin. "I didn't like it."

"So … maybe you're *not* gay."

Noah shook his head. "Men are all I think about. Women don't interest me."

"Top or bottom?"

"What?" Noah's breath faltered, then returned. "I topped."

"Maybe that's your problem."

Noah raised his head and his eyebrows dipped. There was so much confusion behind his eyes. Cole stroked his fingers down the side of Noah's face.

"I'm not interested in bottoming," Noah said.

Cole closed the gap between them and placed his lips lightly on Noah's mouth.

"Maybe you haven't found the right guy yet," he whispered against the pink, puffy lips.

"Maybe," Noah whispered back and then took Cole's mouth. The kiss was hungry, filled with a fierce torrent of emotion that had been denied and hidden for decades.

Cole responded. Waiting to understand the implications be damned. He wanted Noah with a depth of desire that bordered on frenzied. They could talk after.

Noah had too many clothes on.

He yanked at Noah's shirt. "Take all this off."

Noah slipped off the bed. He started with his shirt, discarding it on the floor. His jeans were next. His thick cock emerged hard beneath the fabric of his underwear.

Cole reached for and clung to Noah's bare thigh.

He wanted that cock in his mouth.

He swung his feet onto the floor and slipped his fingers beneath the waistband of Noah's underwear. Noah placed his hand on Cole's head. It was all the encouragement Cole needed.

He stripped Noah's underwear off him.

Cole stroked Noah's cock a few times, then licked and sucked on the cap. The precum leaking from Noah's slit went straight down his throat. Noah's cockhead was wide and the ridge was thick. He eased it into his mouth, twirling his tongue around the domed surface.

Noah groaned and stroked Cole's head.

If he had hair, Noah would be grasping handfuls of it.

He opened his throat and slid Noah's shaft down it. His hard, fat cockhead filled his airway. He dismissed his gag reflex and enjoyed the moment of Noah standing above him.

Cock down his throat.

He'd dreamed of it.

Cole slurped and sucked the full, long surface, and swept his tongue along it as he drew it back past his lips. He released it and looked up at Noah.

"I've been wanting to do that since we were teenagers," Cole said.

He felt Noah's cock pulse in his hand.

Noah's jaw clenched and unclenched. "Me too."

Cole licked Noah's flushed cap. "God ... so much wasted time."

"We're here now."

"I'll thank Debbie later."

Noah laughed. "Don't you dare."

"Mmm." Cole sucked Noah's cock back into his mouth. He worked his hand up and down near the base as he bobbed on the most incredible dick he'd ever sucked.

The best because it was Noah's.

He endeavored to draw more sweet, sultry sounds from Noah's throat.

Noah touched Cole's shoulder. "You'd better stop. You're going to make me cum."

Then why stop?

Cole released the cock he'd been working so hard to please.

"I need to see all of you," Noah said.

That wasn't asking for much. His only item of clothing was his G-string. What had possessed him to climb into bed with Noah half naked, he wasn't sure.

He wrinkled his forehead. Noah had been completely nude. They were both insane.

Cole hooked his fingers in the side straps of his G-string and shimmied the underwear off his hips. His hard cock sprung free. Noah swallowed as he looked down at it.

"Lay back," Noah said.

Cole did what he was told and flopped back on the mattress. Noah took hold of Cole's skimpy underwear and finished removing them. He flung them at the dresser.

He sank to his knees at the side of the bed. Cole opened his legs and Noah crowded in against them. He rested his hands on Cole's hips and kissed the inside of his thighs.

Noah pushed forward and ran his nose from Cole's balls to the tip of his penis, inhaling, so incredibly slow, taking in the entire experience of it.

He kissed Cole's shaft and his gaze met Cole's. "I used to dream about your cock. What it would feel like against my lips?"

"We could have experimented if you had said something."

"I wanted to."

"Why didn't you?"

Noah frowned. "What if our parents had caught us?"

"That's what stopped you from being with me?" Cole ran his hands through Noah's hair. "I didn't say anything because I thought you wouldn't be interested. You acted so bloody straight. I didn't want to lose you as a friend if I tried to tell you how I felt."

Did he dare tell him?

Cole sighed. He felt close to Noah right now.

"I was so in love with you," Cole admitted.

Noah's breathing ramped up. He held Cole's gaze with an unblinking stare.

"Fuck, Cole … you were all I could think about. It was driving me insane."

"So, you pushed me away?"

Noah swept his hands up and down Cole's thighs. "The longing was breaking my heart."

A deep sadness descended on Cole's heart. They'd both been so frightened of their feelings that they had torn their relationship apart. It was the most miserable dismissal of emotions he had ever heard of. They'd been so close to completing each other … and they'd blown it apart.

"You meant everything to me," Noah added as he stroked Cole's cock to keep it hard.

A tear streaked down Cole's face. "Can we fix it … what we had?"

"We can try." Noah rubbed his cheek against Cole's shaft. "I want to try." He turned his face and licked Cole's cockhead. Cole felt a twinge of sorrow when Noah sucked his cock into his mouth like a man who knew what he was doing. This wasn't Noah experimenting. He'd been out there living the life of a gay man without him. They could have been together.

Cole touched Noah's face. "Let me make love to you."

Noah hesitated, then nodded his head.

Cole sat up. "I have condoms and lube in my makeup case." Noah moved aside and Cole was quick to collect everything he needed. While he dug around in his makeup bag, Noah positioned himself face down on the mattress, gripping tight to the pillow as though it was a life preserver.

That just wouldn't do.

"Roll over." Cole climbed onto the bed. "I'm not making love to the back of your head."

Noah was reluctant but eventually flipped over. Cole kissed

Noah's bent knees, then encouraged Noah's legs to open a little wider. He kissed the inside of his thighs. Wider. He kissed the skin on either side of Noah's balls, then sucked one into his mouth. It was full and firm.

"Fuck, Cole," Noah whispered with an exhalation.

Cole swept a finger down Noah's taint and teased the edge of his hole. Noah groaned and squirmed. His hole clenched closed tight.

Cole licked his lips. He needed to taste every bit of him.

"Lift your knees."

"What? Why?"

"Because I am going to take you to the very edge of your endurance."

"Cocky." Noah grabbed behind his knees and lifted them. His legs were shaking before Cole got anywhere near his target. He used his thumbs to expose the tight ring, then leaned in.

"Experienced."

Noah's hole tensed under his tongue.

He would soon fix that. He danced his tongue across the surface of Noah's hole, then licked it with the flat of the stiff, warm—wet muscle. Noah nearly let go of his knees. "Steady, babe."

The word felt strange, *babe*. He'd used it many times … never had he meant it. It was a term of affection he usually used to his advantage. With Noah, though, the affection was real.

"Say it again," Noah said, his hands all over Cole's head, as Cole wriggled his tongue, prodding to be let in. Noah went back to supporting his legs, keeping them spread wide.

Cole kissed Noah's hole. "Let me in, *babe*." He went back to licking and enticing Noah's hole to open for him. He wasn't sure why Noah had asked him to use the word.

But it did the trick.

Noah loosened for him. Cole dipped his tongue in and out of Noah's hole, pushing and retreating. He was able to alternate. Prodding, licking, sucking—kissing.

He kept it up until Noah was calling his name and trembling. Cole reached for the lube. He wasn't finished with Noah yet. He slicked up Noah's hole then slipped a single finger in. Noah clamped down on it, then relaxed. His ass was hot and tight—and soft as velvet inside.

Cole went after Noah's balls as he pumped his finger in Noah's ass. He sucked each one into his mouth and tumbled them over his tongue. He sucked hard and released.

More lube. Two fingers. This time he hooked his fingers and glided across the gland sitting there primed for attention. Noah jumped and moaned.

"What is that?" Noah whispered.

Cole kissed Noah's knee. "You've missed out on so much."

More lube. Three fingers.

Noah groaned, dropped his legs, and bore down on Cole's fingers. Cole pumped faster and deeper, really opening Noah up. Noah began moving his hips in rhythm with Cole's thrusts, fucking himself hard on Cole's fingers. Cole added a fourth and Noah nearly lifted off the bed.

"More," Noah growled.

Cole slipped his fingers from Noah's ass, reached back, and grabbed a condom. He ripped the packet open with his teeth. More lube flowed after he rolled the protection in place.

Cole returned to Noah and gazed down at him. Noah had a wild look in his eyes. His pupils were blown wide. He was panting. He grabbed Cole's upper arms.

"I need you so bad," Noah said.

"This is going to bring us closer." He needed Noah to understand that. This wasn't a random fuck. This meant something. The past sixteen years were about to be wiped out.

"I want that. I'll never push you away again."

Cole believed him. That Noah would never deliberately hurt him again. He lifted one of Noah's legs, took hold of his sheathed cock, and pressed it to Noah's hole. This was monumental. He still loved the man opening for him. Under the hate tormenting his mind, the love had been protected by his heart. He slid in further. Noah cried out sweetly and called his name.

The sound played on repeat in Cole's mind.

He'd never forget it for the rest of his life.

Deep enough to proceed without guidance, Cole supported himself by placing a hand to the left of Noah's chest. He leaned his hips in hard and crept forward as Noah's body accepted him.

Seated against Noah, a single tear escaped down Cole's cheek.

He wiped it away before Noah saw it.

Crazy emotions were swirling around inside him. Love—hate. Sadness—joy. Every feeling he had gone through when Noah ditched him. Every word Noah had just spoken.

The juxtaposition was threatening to tear apart.

He needed to land on one side of the fence or the other.

This side.

I want this with him.

Cole steadied himself on his knees. Each stroke was loving and gentle. Every rock of his hips was met by sighs and moans from Noah's lips. He glanced over at them. Noah's mouth was open, his tongue making the occasional appearance. His beautiful dark eyelashes fluttered in ecstasy. He needed to be closer to that. Cole licked his lips and changed his position.

He could still taste Noah's ass on his lips. Noah looked up at him, challenging him to claim him. To take what he wanted. He watched Noah's eyes. He wanted every piece of this man.

He released Noah's leg and lowered himself onto Noah's chest. Noah lifted his feet off the bed and wrapped his legs around Cole's hips. Cole closed the distance and kissed him.

This is where he needed to be. Chest to chest. Face to face. Lips crushing. Panting—sweating. Pumping and grinding. His cock buried deep in his lover.

His Noah.

Noah met every thrust with an undulation of his own. He cupped the back of Cole's head with both hands. With every ragged breath Noah took, Cole could feel it against his chest. Even the frantic beat of Noah's heart. He could feel it all. This was the closeness he had needed all his life.

Cole lifted away with his arms and raked his cock hard past Noah's prostrate.

Noah gasped and stopped moving.

"Do that again," Noah whispered.

Cole obliged.

"Faster," Noah panted. He dug his fingers into Cole's shoulders. The next few swipes over the gland had Noah scratching long lines down Cole's arms.

It felt good. As if Noah was marking him as his.

He wanted to be his.

He desperately wanted to be his.

As badly as he wanted to claim Noah.

Back and forth, Cole concentrated on hitting his mark.

"Fuck, fuck … fuck." Noah clung harder. His nails dug into Cole's shoulders, then he jerked, his chest rising off the bed, his back bent—and he came hard on his stomach.

Cole was fast to touch it. He ran the heel of his hand through the slickness and smeared it all the way to Noah's right nipple. He lowered his mouth and sucked and licked at the hard nub of slippery flesh. His first taste of Noah's seed—and it was glorious.

Noah ran his hands down to Cole's waist. "Cum in me," he whispered. "I want you to fill my ass and cum in me. I want to feel every inch of your cock."

Cole growled, accepting the challenge. Noah was hungrier than Cole had expected him to be. He was a natural bottom. They were a perfect match.

Cole fell back onto Noah's chest and kissed and licked the side of Noah's throat as he pummeled Noah's hole. He was riding an unimaginable high. Noah was like a drug. He couldn't get enough of him. He drove faster and faster until he grunted and filled the condom.

With each full penetration of Noah's body, sparklers fired off behind Cole's eyes.

His body jerked with sensitivity as he slowed. He hadn't wanted it to end. Three seconds later, he would want to do it again. Again—and again. For the rest of their lives.

Cole closed his eyes and rolled off Noah. He pinched the bridge of his nose. He hadn't meant to think that. It was too much to hope for. They'd agreed to try. But what did that mean?

He turned and clung to Noah's arm. He kissed his shoulder. "Verdict?"

Noah laughed. "I'm definitely gay."

"Told you—right guy."

"You're absolutely the right guy. Where did you learn to do that?"

"Like I said before … experienced."

Those words made Noah frown. "How many?"

Cole rose on one elbow. "So … we're doing that already, are we?"

"I'm curious. Not going to hold it against you."

"You might because I honestly don't know. It's all a bit of a blur."

"The drinking?"

"Partly." Cole drew a line down the center of Noah's chest with one finger. "Partly because I didn't care. Most were meaningless." He pressed his forehead to Noah's shoulder and hid his face. "They weren't you. None of them mattered. You're the only one who would have mattered."

A knot twisted in Cole's stomach. He'd never admitted it to himself before. Even his husband, Darren. He had loved Darren and the sex had been great, but the love they shared had never compared to the love he felt for Noah. Nothing could ever compare to that.

Lying here now with Noah, Darren ceased to matter.

Noah shuffled onto his side, exposing Cole's face. He touched Cole's chin and tipped Cole's face up so Cole's wandering gaze would have to connect with his.

"Is that the truth?" Noah asked.

Cole's brow dipped. "You know it is. I never stopped loving you."

Noah exhaled across Cole's lips. "Even now?"

"After what we just did ... especially now."

Noah pulled Cole to him, kissed his forehead, and tucked Cole's head under his chin. He slung his leg over Cole's hip and tugged him close, folding Cole into an incredible embrace.

"Where do we go from here?" Noah asked.

"We enjoy the rest of the weekend. Go home ... and see what happens."

"What would you like to see happen?"

"Could we date for a while?"

"If that's what you want."

"Yes." Cole smiled against the hollow of Noah's throat. "So ... Noah and Cole are dating."

"We are."

The anxiety circled Cole's heart again. His heart would be torn to shreds if this didn't work out. Maybe they weren't compatible anymore. They'd spent years apart. He barely knew this Noah.

"I'm scared," Cole admitted.

"We'll take it slow."

Those words from Noah's lips were assurance enough. Cole closed his eyes and fell asleep entwined with the man he loved. The man he had loved for over twenty years.

Chapter Six | Noah

Cole had blown Noah's world wide open. Taken him places he'd never imagined existed. Escalated him to heights of thundering reckless desire. His body was still alight with it.

Trixie had a ridiculous nature walk to go on in a few minutes. It had been fascinating to watch Cole transform himself into her. It was a lot more work than Noah had imagined.

Noah wandered into the bathroom where Cole was finishing up.

They'd slept for a couple of hours after making love, then Cole had popped up refreshed as though he hadn't consumed buckets of alcohol. He was making his final check in the mirror.

Cole turned to look at his bare arm in the reflection. He ran his finger down one of the faint pink scratches Noah had left on his skin. "I like it when you mark me."

Noah's cock pulsed and swelled.

He hadn't thought what Cole was eluding to would affect him that way. Noah was still coming to terms with his decision to *come out* for Cole when they went home. He had no intention of dating Cole from the closet. His gaze wandered up and down the scratch.

"Yeah? You like that?"

"Does that turn you on?"

"More than I thought it would."

Cole took a wet cloth, flipped the long hair of his wig aside, wiped the makeup away on a spot on his neck, stepped closer to Noah, and tipped his head to one side.

He tapped his exposed neck.

"Go ahead. Mark me ... make me yours."

The words barely seeped in.

Other than he wanted it. He wanted Cole to be his. He had wanted Cole to be his for the entire time he'd been in high school. And now Cole was offering himself.

Because Cole loved him.

Noah growled and reached for Cole. With both shoulders in his grasp to hold Cole in place, Noah zeroed in on Cole's neck. Long, lean, and smooth. He'd be able to feel the pulse beneath his lips if he paid attention. He latched on. His cock strained against his pants. It was a thrill, knowing Cole wanted him to do this to him. To let everyone know he'd been claimed.

He sucked hard, moving around to make it visible. He took the opportunity to gnaw at Cole's skin when he needed to breathe. There would be temporary marks from his teeth.

Cole groaned and ran his hand into Noah's hair, keeping him in place. Noah changed sides but the other side of Cole's neck was covered in makeup. He switched back, sucking and groaning.

"Fuck," Cole whispered in a breathy voice. "You're going to draw blood."

Noah released Cole's neck and stepped back. Cole was quick to check the mark in the mirror. His face stretched into a wide smile. He turned to show Noah.

Noah ran his fingers over the apple-shaped purple mark. There was no doubt even the people in the back row would see that. People might suspect it was him if they saw them together.

The thought made him even harder—if that was possible.

He couldn't stand it any longer. His cock needed attention. The act of marking Cole had nearly made him cum unassisted. Cole placed his hand on Noah's thrumming bulge.

"Do you need help with that? I can redo my lipstick."

Noah couldn't believe he was going to say this ... to his

childhood best friend.

"Only if you take it with you. I want to mark you on the inside as well."

"Fuck." Cole dropped to his knees and pulled Noah's pants open. He gave Noah's cock its freedom into the cool air-conditioned room but quickly replaced the coolness with his warm mouth. Noah lasted the duration of six shuddering, gasping breaths.

He thought he might never loosen his death grip on the bathroom counter ever again. He hadn't wanted to touch Cole and potentially mess up his drag outfit.

Even the makeup and long blond wig hadn't thrown him off.

It was Cole's mouth.

Cole rose to his feet and licked his lips.

He winked at Noah. "Dinner."

Noah laughed. "No, you're eating proper food tonight."

"You don't approve of my sperm and alcohol diet?"

"Not particularly."

Cole pushed past Noah into the bedroom. "The best I can offer you with the drinking is I'll try." He sat down at the desk, peered in the mirror, and started to patch up his face.

He ran some makeup over his neck but it did little to cover the hickey.

Noah knew Cole had left it exposed like that on purpose. He had makeup that could cover the existence of his eyebrows. A hickey should be child's play.

"That's all I'm asking." Noah approached Cole from behind and placed his hands on Cole's shoulders. "I want to spend time with you again tonight and I want you to remember it."

Cole's shoulders sank beneath his touch.

"I want that too."

Noah didn't ask Cole to do it *for him*. He knew that wasn't the way it worked. Cole had to want to stop drinking. Noah hoped he wasn't setting himself up for heartache.

"You're running late," Noah said.

"They'll wait for me. Are you coming?"

"If you want me to."

Cole smiled at him. "Of course I do."

The walk to the top of the stairs felt strange, as though Noah was headed toward a stage, following along behind the star of the show. He held back as Trixie took the first couple of steps down the stairs. She threw her arms into the air like the Y in YMCA and posed.

"Who's ready to stumble along a nature trail and break their ankles!" his voice rang out. "I know that's where I'm headed with these goddamn heels on!"

There was laughter from below as Trixie descended into the crowd at the bottom of the stairs. Noah figured at that point, it was safe to follow. He'd give Trixie her space to unleash the brash persona that Cole had hidden inside him. The man who had made love to him this morning was in there somewhere, unrecognizable. His Cole was in there.

Debbie bumped up beside him. "Looks like Trixie had a good time last night."

"The show was great."

"No, I meant after." She tapped her neck. "That's quite the hickie. Did she stay out all night?"

Noah sucked in a breath. A part of him was terrified to be found out. The other part of him felt possessive. After all those years of being apart, Cole was his now.

"No. He came straight back to the room last night."

Debbie coughed out a laugh. "You did that?" Her voice was louder and more excited than he had hoped it would be. "I knew it." She shoved Noah's shoulder. "I knew there was something there between the two of you. Naomi owes me twenty bucks."

"You bet on us?"

"It was a sure thing. I couldn't stop myself."

They followed the small group of people outside and headed for the treeline. Trixie was in the lead, bantering and stumbling along as they began their trip into the forest.

"She really is risking a broken ankle in those shoes," Noah said. He was mulling over Debbie's words. A sure thing? Had they been that obvious in high school?

"What made you sure something would happen?" Noah asked.

"Gawd … you two. You were always together. And you had a habit of touching when you spoke to each other. And apart, you'd watch one another all dreamy-eyed down the hall. You waited for each other after school even if you were going separate ways. You'd have these awkward goodbyes and see you tomorrows. It was gag-worthy … honestly."

"I was in love with him … but I couldn't have him."

"Your parents?"

"Exactly."

"That's why you shut him out."

"I couldn't deal with my feelings for him. Knowing he was gay made it worse. Knowing that on some level, he loved me too was agonizing. It would have been so easy for us to slip into something more. A proper relationship. We could have spent the last twenty years together."

"You think it would have lasted that long?"

They wove their way through the trees, down a darkened narrow pathway with roots crossing their route every few steps. Noah watched Trixie. She appeared to be faring well.

Cole was all he had ever wanted. His best friend had been perfect.

"I like to think so," he answered after thinking it over some more.

"So … are you like an item now?"

Cole laughed as the craziest emotion pulsed through him.

Love and joy mixed with worry and trepidation. The joy was winning out. He wanted to be back in their room together so they could talk. So he could get to know this new Cole. This mature experienced Cole.

"Yeah, I guess we are. At least I think so. He asked me to put that mark on him."

"It didn't happen during sex?"

"Nope. In the bathroom before we came down here."

"I'd say that's pretty significant."

Noah pushed a stray cedar bough aside. "He asked me to make him mine before I did it."

"Kinky."

Noah frowned. "Is it?"

"It'll be weeks before that fades. Kinky or not, he's in this for the long haul."

His body released rolling flutters inside his stomach. He *was* going to have to *come out*. Cole wanted to be part of his life. His real life. They'd agreed on dating first, but this was going to move so much faster than either of them expected. He felt that right down to his core.

The worry was whether he was worthy of Cole's attention. Maybe after falling deep, Cole would decide Noah wasn't the same guy inside he once knew. That Noah didn't deserve his love.

"I'm totally in long term. I promised him I'd never push him away again."

"That's a big promise. What if it doesn't work out?"

"I don't want to think that way." Noah did have one concern, though. "A stumbling block might be his drinking. How bad do you think it is?"

"Naomi and I have seen him perform quite a few times over the past couple of years." Debbie wrinkled her brow. "Never saw him without a drink in his hand."

Noah emitted a long sigh. "He promised me he'd try to slow

down."

"That's a big ask. A complicated one. It's a disease he has to conquer. Not simply an easy choice. He has to want it badly enough to fight the craving."

Debbie wasn't telling him anything new.

Noah released a small shuddering breath. "He was still drunk this morning when we had sex. I don't want it to be like that again."

"You want him fully present."

"Okay, I think we're near the river!" Trixie shouted. The group cheered and increased the speed of their feet. That was the main draw, to see the same river that cut through town.

It seemed absurd.

"Of course, I want him to be present," Noah answered. "I want him to feel every emotion I felt this morning. To feel that decades-old yearning partially satisfied."

"Partially?"

"I know there's more to unlock between us. We have some healing to do."

Debbie's excited demeanor relaxed. "You still love him, don't you?"

"I haven't told him yet." Noah looked at the ground. "He said it to me, though."

Debbie gripped his arm. "That is *so* sweet." Her voice was pitched high as though she was speaking to a child. "After all these years. That has to make you feel good."

"It makes me feel scared."

"Scared?"

"Afraid that we'll start dating and he'll realize I'm not good enough. That I'm not loveable anymore." Noah sought closeness with Debbie and placed his head on her shoulder as they stood looking out over the boring river. "I don't want to lose him again."

"I want to say something reassuring, but you're right, you

have some work ahead of you."

Noah turned to watch Trixie after hearing her shriek with amusement. She was in her element. She had the demeanor and wit of a well-seasoned comedian. The group was howling with laughter as she made an analogy comparing herself to a squirrel frantic to gather nuts for the winter.

She'd had *his* nuts in her mouth this morning.

The memory excited Noah's cock.

"Fuck, she makes me hard," Noah admitted to Debbie. "Knowing Cole is under there and how much I want him … god. I hope your wedding reception is so boring, we want to leave."

"She's only doing a few numbers after she emcees the speeches. You'll have plenty of time to do all sorts of nasty things to her tonight."

Noah remembered Cole smearing Noah's nipple with his cum and then licking and sucking it off. He suspected Cole liked it dirty. They had a lot to explore together.

"All right! About face! Back we go! I need a drink!"

Trixie tripped along past the line of people and joined Noah and Debbie. They were headed back to the resort, changing the direction of the group. Now, their threesome was leading.

Trixie linked arms with Noah for support.

"I can take a break," she said. "The peeps are chatting amongst themselves."

"You were really funny," Noah said.

"How would you know? You and Debbie were thick as thieves back here." She smiled at Debbie. "What were you talking about?"

Debbie grinned. "How great the sex was this morning between you two."

Trixie smacked Noah's arm. "Tattle-tale."

"I had some things I needed to talk about," Noah said, bringing the conversation back to reality. Debbie had been a great sounding board.

"Sounds serious."

Noah stopped walking and turned to Cole. "You and I … it is serious. I want to make sure I don't screw it up. It feels like we've been apart forever. I don't want to lose you again."

Cole shook his head. "I'm not going anywhere without you ever again."

"Aw." Debbie patted both their shoulders. She turned to the group. "All right! Follow me! The walk was nice but I have a wedding to get ready for!"

The whole line of people shuffled past them. When they were alone, Noah cupped Cole's face. "I want to kiss you but I know that would mess up your makeup."

"I'll save my lips for you. They're all yours later. Without the lipstick."

Noah trailed the backs of his fingers down Cole's cheek. "Good. You're gorgeous like this and Trixie is growing on me but I like you better without it all."

"That man without it all … is all yours."

Again. Noah's cock stirred because of Cole's words. He'd never thought of himself as being possessive, but then he'd never been in this situation with Cole looking at him with love in his eyes. Cole set a long-nailed hand on Noah's chest and leaned against him.

Noah wrapped an arm around him.

"I love you so much," Cole whispered close to his shirt.

Noah closed his eyes and soaked it in. He wished he could say it back. Tell Cole that seeing him in his office had brought the emotions rushing back. Brought back the love and the need to be with him. Instead. "We should get back to the resort before they start the wedding without us."

"Shit … you're right." Cole pulled a phone out of his dress past his fake double-D breasts. "It's already 1:10. I need to pee before we start this next stretch. I shouldn't have had that coffee."

"I'll come up to the room with you."

They started walking back along the trail. The group was far ahead of them. Noah brushed his hand against Cole's. They linked fingers for the rest of the journey to the resort.

It felt good holding Cole's hand. His fingers had itched to try it since he was probably 12. To touch Cole affectionately. They already had a habit of resting their hands on each other's shoulders, elbows, and knees when they were talking together as though they were meant to be in physical contact with each other. It had taken them almost twenty years to get there.

They'd been as physically close as any two people could be this morning.

Cole had been inside him.

His cock grew and strained against his pants.

He wanted that again. He needed that connection. To stare into Cole's eyes as he filled him time and again. Pumping and grinding—gasping and moaning.

Noah gripped Cole's hand tightly.

He could save it for tonight.

As they stepped onto the resort property, Trixie catapulted back into existence. People were lingering, about to head to the barn structure for the ceremony.

Trixie released Noah's hand and headed for them.

The wedding was beautiful. Even the reception was tolerable … so far. Trixie had emceed the speeches, starting with her outlining the fiasco of events that had brought Debbie and Naomi together as relayed to Trixie by the couple. She had spent 15 of their fleeting minutes memorizing the facts in their room before they went down and joined the wedding ceremony.

Trixie remained at the head table. It wouldn't make sense

for her to sit anywhere else no matter how much they wanted to sit together.

Noah hadn't meant to keep track but he couldn't help it. Trixie had been nursing the same glass of wine all evening. She looked a little on edge but she continued to perform well.

Cole had taken his concerns seriously.

When it came time for her musical numbers, the flamboyant Trixie bounded into the spotlight. She did not disappoint. Between numbers, she bantered with the crowd, making fun of different individuals, couples—people she thought should be couples. Gay men she thought should get together for sex later based on the size of their hands. Noah had no idea where it all came from.

When she finished for the night and the room turned into a dance floor, Trixie became Cole again. Calmer and quieter as he went to stand behind Noah and rub his shoulders.

"I'm exhausted," Cole said as Noah stood from the table. He smoothed out Noah's suit jacket lapels and then slipped his hand into Noah's. "I'm ready to go back to our room."

"I've been waiting all night for you to say that."

Cole smiled. "Now, it's been said."

Noah lifted their joined hands and kissed Cole's fingers.

"Once you're out of drag, I want to hold you for a while."

"That sounds perfect." Cole patted Noah's cheek. "We have a lot to talk about."

Chapter Seven | Cole

Cole tucked tighter into Noah's embrace. "Start at the beginning. Start from when it all went bad between us. I want to know what happened."

"That's kind of a depressing place to start."

Cole craned his neck to look at Noah. "I need to know."

Noah grunted and held Cole close. "When you told me you thought you might be gay my world went from sparkling rockets to a descent into the pits of hell."

"That's dramatic."

"It's what happened. For a flash of a second, I saw us together. Holding hands as we walked to school. Kissing at our locker. Sleeping over at each other's houses and sharing a bed … feeling your skin beneath my fingertips. Making love to you."

"And then that image changed."

"I knew my parents would never allow it. No son of theirs is gay. They raised me better than that, they'd say. I knew they would end up finding out. Someone would talk. Someone who saw us together at school would tell their parents. Then their parents would tell my parents."

"Pits of hell."

"That's what it felt like. I knew I could never be with you the way I wanted."

"My parents would have been fine with it."

"I know … and that hurt too. When you came out—nothing but support."

"I was lucky."

"And I hated you for it. I couldn't stand to be around you."

Cole stroked his fingers along Noah's forearm. "You hurt me so bad. The first time you turned away from me in the hallway and started walking the other way, I felt like I was going to die."

"You recovered. All those interested guys at your locker. Hanging around waiting for you after school. Every time I saw you with one of them, it was like a kick in the gut."

"I *didn't* recover … I masked my pain." Tears collected along the rims of Cole's eyes. "I didn't want any of them. I only wanted you … and you wouldn't even look at me."

Noah was silent. His breathing was broken and shallow.

"I thought you moved on without me."

Cole rose on one elbow. "You pushed me away. But I was right there. Ready to come back if you decided you couldn't live without me. I would've given anything for us to be together again."

"You loved me."

"God, Noah." Cole placed a hand on Noah's chest. "With all my fucking heart."

Noah sucked in a sob. "Fuck."

"If you had known, would it have changed things?"

"I don't know. It might have made things worse."

Cole nodded. "Prom night, you were watching me. I kept heading out into the hallway. I was hoping you would follow me. Grab me, push me against the lockers, and tell me you loved me."

"All I saw was you dancing with that guy, Ryan."

"You remember who it was?"

"How could I not? I saw you kissing under the bleachers and then you took off with him."

Cole picked at the button on Noah's shirt. "He was my first. It was clumsy and it was awkward and the whole time, I kept wishing it was you."

Noah pinched the bridge of his nose as tears streaked down his cheeks.

"Jeezus, Cole, you're killing me."

Cole dusted some tears off Noah's cheeks. "University was the same. No one was ever you."

"My failed gay sexual experience was in university." Noah scrubbed the tears off his face. "Same thing … it wasn't you. When we finished, I didn't want him to touch me. I felt like I had cheated on you. I couldn't get an image of your anguished face out of my head."

Cole looked toward the window.

Best to tell him.

"I was married."

Noah twisted away from him. "What?"

"Three and a half years. Drove him away with my drinking."

"You loved him."

"In my own way." Cole sniffed and a single streak of tears carved a path down his cheek. "It was never going to work long term. I never got over you."

"I ruined everything because I was too scared."

"No. Because you didn't love me the way I loved you."

This time, Noah really shifted. For a second, Cole thought he was going to get up. He tracked Noah with his eyes. He was struggling with something.

Noah settled on his side, one arm tucked beneath his head, and cupped Cole's face in his hand. He stroked his thumb along Cole's temple. "You're so wrong. I loved you with everything I had back then." He wiped away the tears trickling down Cole's cheeks. "And I love you now."

Those two admissions changed things.

Cole shuddered and burst into tears. Decades of regret spilled out of him. He'd been holding onto the despair. He'd dreamed of them being a couple in high school. Holding hands in the halls. Kissing in their bedrooms instead of doing homework. Attending prom as boyfriends. Picking out and going to university together. Sharing a dorm room. Finding their first apartment after they graduated. Decorating it. Supporting each other in their careers. Adopting a pet.

Marriage—home—family.

They'd missed the linear path of it all.

Noah gathered Cole in his arms and held him as they both cried.

They didn't stop until they were worn out.

Cole smiled, sleep and Noah cradling him. Noah had woken him by kissing his eyelids. They'd cried themselves out last night and fallen asleep a tangle of arms and legs.

Noah kissed the tip of Cole's nose.

"Love you," Noah whispered.

Cole soaked in the sound of those words from Noah's lips. He felt as though he was living in a fantasy world where his wildest desires had come true.

"Love you too." It was the word *too* that thrilled him. A response to Noah's love for him. A love he'd discovered Noah had been holding onto as well.

They'd smothered each other with emotions last night. Crying, kissing, clutching—professing their love for one another. It had been electrifying *and* exhausting.

Twenty years worth of *I love you's* in one night.

"I feel like I didn't sleep," Noah said.

"Me either."

Cole brushed his hand over his forehead. It was nice to wake up without a hangover. Especially in the arms of the man who loved him. A man who had claimed him as his.

He'd never done that with anyone before.

It felt right that he and Noah belonged to each other.

"Check-out is in an hour," Noah said.

Cole looked around the room. It was going to take him almost that long to pack up. He had to be careful with everything so as not to damage thousands of dollars of costumes and wigs.

Being a drag queen was expensive. With his husband gone, he was barely scraping by. He'd kept the apartment and Darren had left him with all the furniture. He'd been extremely grateful for that. Darren had a good job as an electrical engineer. He didn't need what they'd bought together.

Once alone, Cole had turned the apartment into a home. Not restricted by Darren's expectations of a clean, orderly environment. Expectations that had fallen on his shoulders.

Cole frowned. He'd been useless at it and Darren had reminded him of that every day. Every one of his shortcomings was constantly picked apart by the man who supposedly loved him.

It hadn't felt like love.

Cole smiled, watching Noah. He was struggling to put one of Cole's costumes onto a hanger to help him out. They were anxious to get home and see where their relationship took them.

This was love.

He pursed his lips, then burst out laughing. Noah was giving a pair of his 3-inch heels a try. Cole rolled out of bed and stood at the end of it to watch Noah's attempt to walk in a straight line.

"You're going to break your ankles."

"No … hang on." Noah took a few shaky strides toward him. "I got this."

Cole hung on to Noah's hands as he stood before him. "You're actually not bad."

"A bit of practice and I could conquer these." Noah licked his lips. "Maybe wear them out."

"You would do that?" Cole grinned. His best friend was insane.

"Sure, why not? They make your ass look great. I need all the help I can get."

Cole hauled Noah to him and grabbed his ass in both hands. "I love your ass." He kissed Noah's cheek. "Especially when it opened so sweetly for me."

Noah groaned. "We have to do that again soon."

"I thought we were going to start by dating. I don't have sex on the first date."

"Please don't tease me about something like that."

Cole stroked Noah's face. "I'll make an exception with you."

"Thank God." Noah looked back and forth over his shoulders. "What do you need me to do? It's only going to take me a few minutes to pack. I suspect you'll be longer."

"How about as I pack each suitcase, you take it down to my car."

"Keys?" Noah stepped out of the shoes as he hung onto Cole's shoulder.

"In my sequin bag over there." It was hanging off the back of the door. "My car is the rusty, silver SUV out front. You can't miss it. It has a big rainbow flag decal on the back."

Noah's brow furrowed. "That's dangerous, isn't it? The flag on your car."

"For me or the car. Because I don't care about the car."

"I meant you."

Cole laughed. "You've seen the way I dress. My clothes scream gay. I've been lucky. Aside from a few snide and homophobic remarks, people generally leave me alone."

It was sweet that Noah worried about him but he'd been out and proud for almost twenty years. This was his life. It was going to be interesting to see how they merged their separate ones.

Noah cupped Cole's face in both hands. "I'm allowed to worry about my boyfriend."

Cole smiled.

Boyfriend.

Six days ago, they had been existing in the hate zone. Their meeting in Noah's office had been tense. He'd phoned the firm and told them he was going elsewhere for legal advice.

"And I appreciate my boyfriend worrying about me."

"But you're fine."

"I'm fine."

Noah kissed him. A short, reassuring kiss. "Then I'll leave it at that."

It was refreshing to be listened to. Not treated like an idiot without an ounce of sense in his head. If Darren hadn't been on board with an open relationship, Cole would have gone crazy. The relationships he'd developed outside his marriage had kept him sane.

What to do with those men now?

He'd need to deal with them soon.

Cole packed the first bag and Noah hauled it out through the door. Cole was right. It took him a while to shower and pack up his belongings but they managed to get out by 11.

Noah leaned against his car. It was a newer expensive model of SUV. Cole suspected Noah might have a town car as well. This one wasn't very lawyer-y. He'd parked it amongst the trees at the edge of the property. There had been barely enough parking for everyone.

Cole handed Noah his phone. "We need to exchange numbers." He accepted Noah's phone. "Put your address in there as well. We should probably know where each other lives."

"I might show up in the middle of the night."

"I *might* let you in if you did."

"Might?"

Cole smirked. "I might even give you a key."

The look on Noah's face. He wanted that. He wanted them to be there in their relationship. Cole walked toward Noah and slung his arms around Noah's neck.

He kissed Noah's cheek.

"Do you want that? To be able to come to me … and get your ass satisfied?"

Noah's chest rose and fell so fully that Cole felt it against his ribs. The exchange of keys would mean more than that. Most of the time, he would want to simply be held by Noah. To spend hours talking. Reminiscing—planning. Uncovering secrets. Exchanging words of love.

"My ass is yours anytime you want it."

Cole groaned as his cock swelled. "Goddamn, you make me hard."

"I used to masturbate to pictures of you."

What?

Cole's cock pulsed.

"High school?"

"Yeah."

"Before or after I told you I was gay?"

Noah grinned. "Before."

"Jeezus." Cole pressed his hips against Noah, pinning him to his car. He pumped his hips, grinding his hard cock against Noah's stiffening one. He shoulder checked. No one was around.

Before.

Noah had jerked off to him when they were still friends.

The image of that ignited an inferno.

Cole ran his hands into Noah's hair, kissed him, and increased the pressure of his cock. Noah gripped Cole's ass and tugged him into a faster rhythm. The pace he set transported Cole into another dimension. He was no longer in public. This was just them.

The kiss became a frantic attack on each other, gasping, groaning, swallowing air, tongues fighting for dominance. His hands were everywhere. Noah's hair. His neck. His chest.

Cole thrust harder.

Noah shivered and groaned into his mouth.

Oh, Christ.

Cole bit Noah's bottom lip and released pulse after pulse of cum into his pants. He kept Noah pinned to the car until his body slowed. He unbuttoned and opened the front of Noah's jeans and covertly slipped his hand past the waistband of Noah's underwear.

Noah's cock was hard and the material near the head was damp. Cole wrapped his hand around it and pulled up. Noah let out a strangled moan and let his arms drop to his sides.

"Keep your arms there. Don't touch me."

Noah's gaze locked onto him. Absolute carnal desire lit up his eyes. Cole tugged on Noah's cock. "Keep looking at me. I want to see your eyes when you cum."

There were a few times when Noah looked as if he was about to close his eyes. His expression was almost pained when he spilled into Cole's hand.

Cole lifted his hand, locked eyes with Noah, and licked his hand clean. His palm and every one of his fingers, dragging his tongue and lips over his skin.

"You taste so good. I'm going to savor you my whole drive home."

Noah swallowed and pulled Cole toward him. He was quick to take Cole's mouth and search every crevice of it, his tongue sweeping over every surface, chasing the taste.

His boyfriend was famished.

They'd have to explore that desire of Noah's to taste himself.

Cole shifted his weight to one hip. The cum in his pants was wet and tacky. Luckily, he had no hair for it to stick to. "I need to go to the washroom and clean up."

"I'll come with you."

Cole raised an eyebrow. "Okay." He walked to the parking lot and opened the back of his car. Luckily, the suitcase with his day clothes was closest to the door. He opened it and removed a pair of pants and a G-string. He tucked the underwear into the pants and rolled them in his hands.

They bounced up the stairs of the resort and headed for the public washroom. Once inside, Noah shoved Cole into a stall and closed and locked the door. He took Cole's clean clothes from him and hung them on a hook on the back of the door.

Cole knew where this was going. He'd planned to get a wet paper towel to clean himself up, This was better. Noah fell to his knees and pulled Cole's pants and underwear off his hips. He helped Cole step out of them, then folded them neatly and set them on the floor.

God, he's beautiful down there.

Noah started with his balls, his nose pressed to the bottom of his shaft which was stiffening more by the second—sucked into the depths of the warmth of Noah's mouth, his tongue swirled around the first sensitive sac. Stretch—suck—pop. The other one received the same treatment.

Cole touched the top of Noah's head. Noah licked the underside of his shaft like he was trying to keep a melting popsicle at bay. Each swipe of Noah's tongue landed somewhere different, licking away any evidence of the cum he'd been coated in.

There was going to be more.

Noah took Cole's cock into his mouth. Sucking, licking—and moaning, Noah brought Cole to climax. Cole had to brace himself against the wall of the bathroom stall. The strength of Noah's mouth had made him light-headed. Noah rose to his feet and closed his mouth over Cole's.

They hummed against each other as they explored. It was a

slow journey, taking in all of the sights, sounds—and tastes. They collapsed against the stall wall but continued.

Cole wasn't sure how long they were in that bathroom.

Finally worn out, they clung to each other, foreheads pressed together, staring at the floor.

"I love you," Noah said.

"With my entire heart," Cole answered.

"We should go home."

"Pants first."

Noah smiled. "If we were in the same car, I might insist you didn't put them on."

Cole smacked Noah's arm. "Exactly how kinky are you?"

"I have no idea."

Chapter Eight | Noah

There was no other answer to that question. *I don't know*. Noah thought about it for the entire first three hours of the journey home. He could see Cole's car ahead of him. He'd insisted on following when Cole expressed that his car might not make it back to Kelowna.

Exactly how kinky are you?

Probably not much, but he had a few things he liked. What they'd done on the edge of the parking lot and in the resort's main bathroom had ticked a lot of boxes. He wasn't afraid of cum, that's for sure. Even his own. Being in reasonably private public spaces had wound him up. He liked being in public but didn't like the idea of someone catching them.

And he loved it when Cole talked dirty to him.

Noah smiled. He knew the story about using pictures of Cole to get off would have the desired reaction. He'd stopped using pictures of Cole as soon as they weren't talking to each other anymore. Especially because the hate started to build. He'd had one anger wank but he hadn't liked it.

He'd torn up all the photos of Cole and thrown them out.

It was raining lightly. The glow from his headlights stretched out in front of him, reflecting on the wet midday pavement. He was upset Cole didn't have a newer car. They could've been talking to each other hands-free for the entire journey instead of sitting on their own.

Noah slowed as Cole pulled into a rest area, and followed him.

He parked his car beside Cole's.

"Everything all right?" He walked to Cole's driver's side.

"Car's fine." Cole got out of his car and stretched. "I needed some fresh air." He walked toward Noah. "And a kiss from my boyfriend." He wrapped his arms around Noah's neck and brushed his nose on Noah's. "I think a kiss alone might sustain me."

Noah blinked as a multitude of raindrops hit his cheek. "It's raining."

"Then you better take me somewhere dry."

Noah looked into the windows of Cole's car. The entire space inside was stuffed with luggage. He took Cole's hand and led him over to his car. Cole slipped into the back seat.

"Come on." Cole waved his hand, motioning for Noah to follow him. There was no harm in it. The rest stop was practically empty. He slid into the backseat right into Cole's arms. He slammed the door closed and dove into the pool of desire infusing his backseat.

Noah tipped Cole back and climbed on top of him. As their passion began to run away from them, Cole burst out laughing. So much so that he was shrieking and pounding on Noah's chest.

Noah grinned. "What the hell has gotten into you?"

Cole sucked in a gasp and wiped a tear from his cheek. "Oh, my god." He blew out a long breath and fanned his face with his hand. "I just remembered, I hate backseat makeout sessions."

"And that makes you break out in a giggling fit?"

"Can't help it. We should have spent hours in the backseat of your old beater in our senior year. Then I'd be able to take stolen moments in the back of a car more seriously."

"And ...."

Cole cleared his throat. "Maybe it's not funny."

"Okay, now you have to tell me."

"It's about Ryan."

Noah rolled his eyes and sat up. That was the end of their tumble in the car. "Let me guess, you lost your virginity to prom night Ryan in the backseat of a car."

Cole pushed himself up off the upholstery until he was upright.

"His dad's four-door sedan."

"And how was it?"

Cole smiled. "My head kept bashing against the door handle. I thought I was going to end up with a concussion. We had no idea what we were doing. The first ten minutes consisted of him rutting and grunting nowhere near my hole. His dick just kept bouncing off my balls."

Cole stroked Noah's face. "That's the part that got me laughing."

"So, backseats are out."

"Unless you want your car to smell of ass and cum. His dad had to have known what we got up to in the back of his car. He probably had to burn it. We came all over the seat."

Noah leaned in close to Cole. "I would've made our first time special."

"Like rose petals and heart-shaped bed special?"

Noah laughed softly. "Not sure my allowance would have covered that." He reached for and held Cole's hand. "There would have been candles." He smiled. "And fresh sheets."

"Not the Space Wars ones?"

"Maybe, but they'd be clean." Noah brushed his thumb across the top of Cole's hand. "Chocolate-covered strawberries. I would have fed them to you. Traced your skin with them."

Cole leaned his head on Noah's shoulder. "That sounds amazing."

"I would have made love to you so sweet and slow. Worshipped every bit of you. Drawn circles with my tongue all over your body. Tasted every fold and crease. Made you gasp for breath, every molecule of your body on fire. I would have filled you with careful, caressing strokes.

"Then we would have cum together—united in love." He lifted Cole's hand to his lips and kissed it. "That's what I would have done for you."

He wasn't surprised to see that Cole was crying.

"Noah … that's beautiful."

"I dreamed about it most nights for months. It's when I realized I was in love with you."

Cole searched Noah's eyes. "How could we have been so stupid?"

"We were kids."

"But we were in love."

"Too late to go back," Noah said. "Let's enjoy the fact we've found each other again."

"And we are not messing it up this time."

"We need to stay honest with each other. No secrets this time."

Cole nodded and looked at the seat. Noah didn't like the slump of Cole's shoulders. It was scaring him. He slipped his hand from Cole's. "What is it?"

"I want to tell you everything. I know I need to tell you everything." Cole's gaze rose and fixed on Noah. "Because you mean *everything* to me."

There was a real possibility …

"You're still with your husband."

Cole furrowed his brow and shook his head. "No. We haven't been together in a long time."

"Then what?"

Cole set his hand on Noah's thigh. "Darren, my husband, and I had an open arrangement."

What?

Noah shot back against the doorframe. This couldn't be real. Cole couldn't be asking for this from him. "That's what you want? You want to see other people?" If he could've climbed out of the car, he would have. He wasn't sure he wanted to hear the answer.

Cole lunged forward and put his hand on Noah's chest. "No … God, no."

"Then why are you telling me?"

Cole swallowed hard. "Because I've been with some of those guys for years."

That was going to take a second to sink in. Cole with multiple men … for years. Why? Why would he do that? He'd heard of open relationships but he'd never understood them.

"Some are married. Some are single," Cole continued. "It was a way to get away from Darren when I wasn't working. Some have come and gone … others have stuck around."

Noah could feel the pulse beating below his jawline.

"So, how does this affect us?"

"I want to be honest about my life. It wasn't all casual sex."

"Do you have feelings for any of these guys?"

Cole chewed on his bottom lip. "The ones I'm with now … I love them as friends."

"But you love them."

Cole shuffled closer to Noah. "Not the way I love you. It doesn't compare."

"So … what happens with these guys? Now that we're together?"

"I'll meet each of them for coffee and tell them I've found my forever guy."

"Just like that."

Cole clenched Noah's shirt. "You are the absolute love of my life. I didn't want to hide this from you. We're not doing that anymore. No more keeping the truth from each other. If either one of us had spoken up all those years ago, things would be so different for us now."

Noah relaxed. Cole was right. They couldn't make the same

mistakes again. They could discuss this in more detail later about why Cole felt the need to have more than one relationship.

"How do you think things would be different if we had followed our hearts and spoken up?"

Cole leaned against him. "We'd have our own home." He smiled. "With a dog."

"Just a dog?"

Cole gripped Noah's arm and hid his face. "And five kids."

Noah coughed out a laugh. "Not four. Not six. But precisely five."

"Lucky seven with two parents."

Noah kissed Cole's head. "I could do five."

Cole pulled away. The topic had become too serious. It was too early to be talking about children. "We should get going. I want to be home now."

Noah took a deep breath. Those few minutes had been an elevator marathon of emotions. He wanted to be home too. His home wasn't as warm and cozy as Cole's might be—but it was home.

And he had paperwork to catch up on.

On the first day back at work after the weekend, Noah found himself swamped and crying uncle to no avail. Carol was off sick and might be out for a while, so he had to take on her workload. If he didn't, all his case files would grind to a halt. The office promised him they would find a sub.

But for today, he was on his own.

Yesterday, he'd followed Cole to his apartment, kissed him, and told him he'd call him later. He had a bunch of paperwork to get through but he would phone him as soon as he finished.

That's *not* how it worked out.

He'd fallen asleep on his paperwork around 11 and hadn't

woken up until 2 in the morning. It had been too late to call Cole and he felt terrible about it.

He looked at his phone. There were four unread text messages from Cole that he hadn't gotten around to looking at yet. He would. Just not yet. Maybe when he had a quiet minute to himself.

The next time he looked at his phone, it was 8 pm. He'd missed dinner entirely. He leaned back in his chair and opened the text messages from Cole. There were 8 now.

And 4 missed phone calls.

11:58 pm

Cole: <I guess you fell asleep?>

12:03 am

Cole: <Hello?>

8:23 am

Cole: <Good morning.>

8:25 am

Cole: <Love you.>

10:56 am

Cole: <I guess you're busy.>

4:17 pm

Cole: <What's happening?>

6:48 pm

Cole: <So what? One weekend and that's it?>

7:37 pm

Cole: <Fuck you.>

Noah nearly dropped his phone.

No.

He opened Cole's profile on his phone and pressed the call button. It rang fifteen times as his heart thrashed around frantically in his chest, and then went to Cole's voicemail.

<We're sorry. This mailbox is full. Please try again later.>

Shit.

He nearly threw his phone across the room in frustration.

He couldn't lose Cole like his. Not over something as stupid as a few unreturned text messages.

He needed to find him and explain.

Noah collected his keys and dashed for the elevator. He could absolutely understand why Cole was pissed. He hadn't meant to ignore him but when he got in the zone with work, there was very little that could distract him. He'd muted his phone so he wasn't interrupted.

While in the car, he played the one message Cole had left.

"I get it. We came at each other fast. We shouldn't have. We should have left things in the past." A pause. *"My love for you is real. I'm sure you believed yours was when you told me. But now you've had a while to think about it. Realized you were mistaken. We'll just go our separate ways."* The sound of Cole crying. *"Fuck, Noah. I'm going to miss you now that I've tasted your lips. You were my best friend and I love you so much. I know I'm a fuck up."*

Then the message ended.

Noah wiped the tears from his cheeks.

Cole, a fuck up?

Never.

He pulled up outside Cole's apartment. The intercom buzzed four times but no one answered. He tried it again but nothing. Either Cole was home and avoiding him or he wasn't home. He opened a search engine on his phone. The local gay bar had a website with listings of the events happening every night. It was possible Cole was working tonight.

They were closed on Monday.

He had no idea where Cole was.

Noah sat on the steps of Cole's complex. He settled in to wait. He tried Cole's phone number again. Still no answer. He switched to texting.

Noah:<Cole, where are you? I'm at your place.>
Noah:<I love you. Please answer.>

Noah: <I love you so much. I'm sorry I didn't answer you.>
Noah:<It'll never happen again. I promise.>
Noah:<You're my best friend. I'm going to love you forever.>
Noah:<Please, please, please come back to me.>
Noah:<I'll never stop loving you. Please. I need to hold you.>
Noah:<You are the furthest thing from a fuck up.>

He sat there for almost three hours. Cars and people came and went. Some asked if he was all right. If he needed into the building. Was he waiting for someone?

Noah:<You're my everything.>
Noah: <I love you more than my need to breathe.>

A black, high-end, two-door sports car pulled into a parking space near the door. Noah could make out two figures through the tinted windows. It was definitely Cole in the passenger seat.

Noah rose to his feet.

Was this one of the guys Cole had told him about?

After a few minutes, both doors of the car popped open. A blond guy with his long hair in a knot emerged from the driver's side. Cole nearly fell out of the passenger door. The good-looking guy ran around to Cole's side of the car and assisted him in standing. They were both laughing.

Noah held his breath.

It was just a few missed text messages. That's all it had taken to send Cole into another man's arms? He refused to believe that. They were destined to be together. They'd claimed each other.

He strode toward the car.

Cole caught sight of him. "Noah!"

Noah held back, standing just out of Cole's reach. Cole was shrieking with laughter at top volume and barely able to stand, calling Noah's name over and over again.

Shit-faced was the word that sprung to mind.

Noah wanted to assess the situation before he stepped into the middle of it. He wasn't above fighting someone for Cole but he'd prefer not to.

The guy Cole was with, despite the long hair, was obviously wealthy. His beard was trimmed to perfection and his clothes had not come off any rack Noah had ever encountered. The expensive shoes on his bare, tanned feet and flashy gold watch completed the picture.

Noah felt like he had nothing on this guy.

Cole was dressed in street clothes. A flamboyant summer outfit that screamed gay, but street clothes. At least he'd had the sense to keep himself from going out in drag to drink.

The guy smiled at Noah. "I take it you're Noah."

Noah crossed his arms. "I am."

"Thank God. Cole won't shut up about you."

"And you are?"

"Sorry." The guy extended his hand but Noah ignored it, kept his arms crossed.

"I'm Patrick," the guy continued. "I've known Trixie for years. My husband, Charles, and I launched a rescue mission when she called." He adjusted the white sequin purse back onto the shoulder of Cole's purple romper. "She was like this when I picked her up at Deckers bar. I sat with her for a bit. Tried to find out what was going on. Your name came up … a lot. And something about her not drinking anymore. Which obviously didn't work out for her tonight."

"Thank you for looking out for him." Noah took over in supporting Cole. The guy seemed harmless enough. Sounded like he was just a friend of Cole's. Nothing more.

Noah struggled to support Cole. He was like a dead weight, his legs barely supporting him. He looked down. Cole wasn't wearing any shoes. That was probably a blessing. 3-inch heels wouldn't be helping the situation. Where they were was anyone's guess.

Luckily, Cole had calmed down, mumbling something Noah couldn't understand.

"She had some luck with a 12-step program a few months back. Maybe she could revisit that. There's even a queer one I think. I can ask my husband. He's more up on this than me."

"I'll look into that but Cole probably remembers the details of the meeting."

"Yeah, probably." Patrick pointed at Cole's purse. "His keys are in there. I checked. The plan was to stay with him overnight. It wouldn't be the first time I've held his head over a toilet."

"How often does this happen?" Noah shifted Cole's weight. He'd fallen silent, his head hanging down against his chest, one of his arms slung around Noah's neck.

Fuck, he's drooling. This was bad.

"You haven't known Cole for long?"

"We grew up together. Just reconnected."

"Ah ... that's what he was going on about. It all makes sense now." Patrick walked to the driver's door. "Maybe he'll slow down with you in his life. He thought for sure you'd dumped him."

Noah shook his head. "I'd never do that."

"You say that but you're taking on a lot." Patrick reached over the center console of his car. "I have her shoes." He looked out through his open door at Noah. "Maybe I'll hold on to them for now. Your hands are full." He leaned against his car. "Trixie is a whirlwind of a force to be reckoned with. We're here to help if you need anything, but I don't envy you."

Fear and resignation filled Noah's chest. *I don't envy you.* It felt like his ribcage opened up and dumped his heart into his stomach. He hugged Cole to him.

He could do this for Cole. Together, they could weather this.

"I know I'm taking on a lot. But he's worth it." Noah started walking Cole toward the door. The stairs were difficult. "Thanks again," he called over his shoulder.

It was a struggle to retrieve Cole's keys and hold him up. After a few tries, they finally stumbled into Cole's apartment. Noah hauled him toward where he thought he'd find the bedroom. The state of Cole's living room shocked him a little. It was like a glorified drag closet.

He took a second to look at everything, then carried on.

No sooner had he arranged Cole on the bed to get his clothes off, than Cole rolled over and threw up on the carpet. Noah was quick to get his clothes off after that. He dug around in Cole's drawers and found something suitable for him to sleep in.

After dressing him, he hauled Cole up and dragged him to the bathroom. Cole was quick to tuck his knees under him and cling to the toilet bowl.

In between bouts of throwing up, Noah fed him glasses of water.

They were in there for hours. It broke Noah's heart to watch Cole intermittently fall asleep with his cheek on the edge of the porcelain. Then violently sit up and release more vomit.

Noah caressed Cole's bristly head.

Cole lifted his head. "Noah?"

"I'm right here, babe."

"I'm so sorry. I screwed up."

"No, I'm sorry, I didn't answer your texts and phone calls."

"I thought you changed your mind about us."

"I would never do that. I'm in this forever."

Cole turned and looked at Noah. "Even like this?"

"I'll do everything I can to help you with this. But ultimately, this is your fight."

Cole put his face back down on the edge of the toilet bowl. "I'm so tired."

"Do you think we can risk putting you in bed?"

"I'm empty. Pretty sure even that water came up."

"Okay, let's go." Noah helped Cole off the floor. Cole needed to drain his bladder. Noah had to keep him from tipping over and keep his stream hitting the bowl. He stayed close as Cole stumbled into the bedroom. Cole frowned when he looked at the vomit on the carpet.

"Fuck."

"Don't worry. I'll clean it up."

Cole collapsed on the bed. "You don't have to do that."

"I don't mind."

"Okay. There's a well-worn carpet cleaner in the front hall closet."

Noah arranged Cole on his side. Recovery position. And climbed in behind him. It made him sad that Cole owned his own damned carpet cleaner. Probably for nights like this.

He tucked close to Cole, pulled Cole's back up against his chest, and hugged him. He buried his face at the back of Cole's neck. He wasn't going to leave this man.

Ever.

When Noah woke, Cole was gone from the bed. He could hear him retching in the bathroom. He swung his feet out of bed and went to check on him.

"Anything coming up?"

"No, just a whole lot of dry heaving."

"Have you had some aspirin?"

"No. They're in the medicine cabinet. And anti-nausea stuff. Can you grab me both?"

Noah fussed with the family-sized bottles and dispensed the pills. He filled the water glass with water and handed everything to Cole.

Cole paused for a second, still kneeling in front of the bowl.

"Cross fingers, these stay down." He tossed the pills back and swallowed the whole glass of water.

"Do you want me to make you some toast?"

"That would be awesome." Cole reached out for Noah's hand. Noah grabbed the clammy, cool flesh of Cole's hand and squeezed. "I've been worse. Thank you for staying, though."

"I've got you," Noah said.

"I'm going to try to stop."

"Patrick said you had success with 12-step before."

Cole screwed up his face. "You met Patrick?"

"You called him. He drove you home."

"I don't remember." Cole shook his head. "I hate when I black out like that. I usually wake up in a strange bed or propped against my front door."

That struck a spike through Noah's heart. That Cole had been wandering around out there on his own. Ending up who knows where. No one looking out for him.

His precious best friend deserved better than that.

"Apparently, you told him all about us," Noah said.

Cole smiled. "I probably annoyed the hell out of him. Patrick is a nice guy. His husband, Charles, too once you get used to him. They both work at a winery. One of my favorites."

"Maybe we can get together with them sometime."

"I'd like that but those two are wine connoisseurs. Might not be the best friends for us."

"You're serious about this … not drinking."

"I'm serious about working the steps. I want to stop creating chaos in my life." Cole had to hold onto the counter to stand. "I need to brush my teeth. Stuff growing in there."

"I'll leave you to it."

Noah walked out to the kitchen. It was a mess of utensils and small appliances. The usual kettle and toaster. But Cole also had an air-fry toaster oven, a mixer, a food processor, and a deep fryer. For a guy who didn't eat much, he sure had a lot of tools to create meals and baked goods.

Noah made the toast. As he was plating it, Cole wandered into the kitchen.

"You have a lot of cooking stuff."

"Darren used to make me cook. I should probably throw it all out."

"*Make* you?"

"Yeah, when I quit my day job, he came down on me hard. It was suddenly my responsibility to keep the *home hearth* burning. AKA do everything around here."

Noah's gut clenched. "Did he abuse you?"

Cole lifted a piece of toast. "He never hit me. Just made me feel like shit. I had nothing else to do all day according to him. I was never able to live up to his expectations."

"Were you doing drag then?"

"Yeah, it was my release."

"I'm sure that takes up a lot of time all on its own."

"It does. I'm always having new outfits and wigs made. I have numbers to practice. And that doesn't include the business side of it. I've managed to make it into a full-time job."

"But that didn't matter to him."

"He never supported my drag. Just tolerated it."

"But it's such a huge part of who you are."

"He didn't care who I was most of the time. And then other times, he could be so loving and tender with me. It used to mess with my head, not knowing day to day where we were at."

"Who broke it off?"

"He did. Told me I was useless as a husband … and that I was a drunk." Cole played with the toast in his hand. "He was right. The drinking on top of everything made me pretty useless."

"You're not useless." Noah stepped close to Cole and wrapped his arms around Cole's waist. He kissed his nose.

"You're amazing and you're perfect and you're mine."

Cole smiled. "You're biased. You knew me when I was more put together."

"School?"

"The first part of our lives together. I remember meeting you in kindergarten. You were as quiet as me. You used to let me share the trains with you. We would play with them together."

"Then Grade 3, we joined a soccer team."

Cole laughed. "What a disaster. I was afraid of the ball."

"We practiced together until you improved your skills."

"You got me through Algebra 9," Cole remembered.

"You got me through Biology 11."

Cole lowered his head to Noah's shoulder. "We've always been there for each other."

"That's not going to change now that we're back together."

"I'm feeling amazingly normal but I'm exhausted." Cole lifted the plate of toast. "I'll take this with me to bed. You can go home. It's almost 7. I'm sure you're working today."

"I can take the day off."

"Don't mess up your career for me." Cole gave Noah a light shove. "Go. I'll see you later."

"Are you working tonight?"

"I have Amateur Night at the bar. It starts at 8."

"I'll meet you there. Take you home after."

"I promise I won't drink."

"That's your choice. I'm not going to tell you what to do."

"Okay, but I'll go to a meeting later this morning."

Noah cradled Cole's face in his hand. "I'm proud of you."

"Why? I haven't done anything yet?"

"You've made the decision. That's huge."

Noah wanted to gather Cole up in his arms, haul him back to bed, and make love with him. Make him cry out and gasp for breath. He closed his lips over Cole's. The kiss was tender.

Not demanding. They could save that until later tonight. He had every intention of driving Cole to sexual distraction tonight. Maybe find out more about each other.

"I love you," Cole whispered against his lips.

"With my whole being, you're the one my heart beats for."

Cole giggled. "Who knew you were such a romantic."

"I used to whisper *I love you* to you when you were asleep."

"I wish I had woken up and heard that."

Noah brushed his thumb across Cole's lips. "I hated when we slept in separate sleeping bags when we had sleepovers."

"Me too. I had to stop myself from climbing into yours with you."

"We were so close to connecting."

"Young love."

"We owe Debbie a *Thank You* note."

Cole brushed his lips across Noah's chin and up his jawline to behind his ear. He kissed the sensitive skin. "We'll take them out for dinner," he whispered.

Noah's breath rocked him back and forth, his inhalations and exhalations heavy, dragging in and out. He wasn't going to be able to wait. His cock had never been so hard.

"Are you sobered up?"

"Stone cold."

Fuck.

The plate clattered out of Cole's hand onto the counter, dumping the toast onto the floor. It crunched beneath Noah's feet as he swept in and attacked Cole's mouth.

Noah lifted Cole onto the counter. Their lips locked. Cole clawed at Noah's shirt until he pulled it up. They broke contact for long enough to get the shirt off over Noah's head.

Noah tipped his head back in ecstasy when Cole raked his fingernails down Cole's arms. The sting was exhilarating. He surged at Cole, taking his mouth again. His hands worked loose the silk sleeping shorts he'd put on Cole earlier. Cole lifted his ass so Noah could take them off.

They hit the floor at Noah's feet.

It was a short distance from Cole's mouth to his cock. Noah sucked the full hard length into his mouth. The cap bounced against the back of his throat. He'd dreamed of having Cole's cock down his throat. Even as an adult, he'd formulated an adult version of Cole to suck on.

He worked Cole's cock in and out of his mouth. He wanted it to be hard and ready. His ass was aching for him. It was a deep ache from his hole right up through his guts.

He needed it filled.

He needed Cole close to him again. As close as they could possibly be.

Cole raked his hand into Noah's hair.

"There are some condoms and lube under the bathroom sink."

Noah sprung toward the bathroom. He had to dig behind some towels but he found what he was looking for. He had the condom wrapper open when he hit the kitchen.

Cole was standing in the center of the floor, stroking himself.

Noah forged his way back into Cole's mouth with his tongue as he rolled the condom onto Cole's cock. As soon as it was in place, Cole spun Noah around to face the cupboards.

Cole covered Noah's back with his chest, his arms wrapped around Noah's waist, his hands busy releasing Noah's dress pants. They soon landed on the linoleum.

Noah kicked them away. They ended up in front of the stove in a heap. Cole's lubed thumb came in contact with the skin just above his hole. Noah spread his legs and bent forward, supporting himself on the counter. He groaned as Cole pushed his thumb all the way in.

He wasn't being as gentle as he had been at the resort.

Noah mentally ticked off another box in his head.

It was possible, he liked it rough.

He lowered his head onto the counter, nearly hyperventilating, as Cole hammered his thumb into him. Wouldn't that be entertaining if he passed out.

The slim thumb slipped from his ass. It was replaced by a round, hard cap.

Jeezus.

Cole speared him with one slow, smooth thrust.

"You were hungry for it," Cole said. "Didn't want to keep you waiting."

Noah grunted in response. Each rock of Cole's hips jammed Noah's hip bones against the countertop and nearly knocked the air out of him. Speech wasn't going to be possible.

"Don't touch yourself," Cole said.

Not a problem. Noah needed his hands to support his body, to keep from being pummeled into the countertop completely. Each thrust nearly lifted him off his feet.

Cole slowed and adjusted his grip to protect Noah's hips.

"So hungry," Cole growled. "Your ass just fell open for me."

Noah shivered all the way down his spine. That tone in Cole's voice. The words. A whooshing, buzzing sound ran through his head. His cock pulsed and jumped. He wanted more.

"Harder," he managed.

Cole slapped Noah's ass—hard. The sting left by Cole's hand made Noah hiss. A sweat broke out on his forehead. He needed more of that. Another box ticked.

"What my baby wants, he gets."

Noah grunted each time Cole closed in against him. Faster and faster. Harder. The grunts turned into frantic, lust-filled cries. Mewling so loud he was sure the neighbors could hear.

Nothing had ever felt this good.

Cole pulled out and drooled some more lube down his ass

crack onto Noah's hole. He used his fingers to work it in, teasing Noah with the inadequacy of his long, slim digits.

He used his thumb to pull down and stretch Noah's hole open.

"Such a pretty boy pussy."

Noah nearly came.

Box—tick, tick, tick.

Cole slid back in and pumped slowly, popping his cockhead in and out of Noah's hole. It was infuriating. Noah wanted to feel it high in his guts.

Cole increased his pace until Noah was once again bashing against the edge of the countertop. This time, Cole's fingers weren't there to save him. Cole leaned down and kissed the center of Noah's back, wrapped his arms around Noah's waist, and buried himself deep.

"I'm gonna cum," Cole whispered, then slid out of Noah's ass.

Noah couldn't see what Cole was doing, but Cole had one hand on Noah's lower back, he was groaning, and Noah could hear the unmistakable sound of someone jerking off.

Cole clutched Noah's hip and grunted, and warm droplets hit Noah's lower back. Cole had taken off his condom and emptied himself on Noah's skin.

He wished he could see the mess.

Noah kept his head down and waited. His own cock was aching. He was sure there was a puddle of precum on the floor at his feet.

Cole ran his hand all over Noah's back, scooping and collecting. Then Cole moved his arm around Noah's hip and grabbed Noah's cock. He was using his own cum as lube.

Noah shuddered and closed his eyes.

Oh, my god.

So good.

He pumped his cock into Cole's hand. Cole held firm and

kissed the back of Noah's neck as Noah pleasured himself in Cole's fist. His breath was so hot.

It felt dirty to use Cole's hand like that.

He increased his pace.

So dirty.

Fuck.

He spilled all over Cole's hand. He gasped and shuddered as his body pulsed out the last few drops. Cole slid his fist all the way up his shaft—tight. It almost made Noah whimper.

"Turn around," Cole whispered.

When he turned, a twinge sped through Noah's back. He'd been bent forward over that counter for a long time. Any pain he felt faded into the background as Cole's incredible green eyes caught his attention. Cole raised his coated fist and licked it like it was a frosted cinnamon bun.

Lick after lick of white cum was collected by Coal's tongue.

Noah couldn't take his eyes off Cole's mouth.

He was ready when Cole lowered his hand and leaned in to kiss him. The wad of fluid Cole pushed into his mouth was unexpected. Cole urged it further into Noah's mouth with his tongue.

Cole pulled away. "That's from both of us."

Noah swallowed. Combined. The concept gave him an incredible thrill. Together in his mouth. He ran his tongue over his gums and down the sides of his cheeks.

Together.

He grasped Cole's face in his hands and kissed him.

Cole had given him exactly what he needed.

They were in this together.

Chapter Nine | Cole

Cole twiddled his thumbs as the 12-step meeting started. It had been over three months since he'd been in the room. Last time, he'd reached his four-month mark. The time before that was two months. The time before that one month. It was a slow progression but maybe this would be the time. Maybe this time he'd finally kick the addiction. Or at least, hold it at bay.

He crossed his legs and set his heeled foot tapping in the air. The conversation after they'd cleaned up in the kitchen had been different than anything that would have happened with Darren.

He'd reminded Noah he was going to a meeting this morning.

"I'm proud of you, but you don't need to tell me when you're going. I'm not going to check up on you. You're an adult. I trust you to make the decision that is right for you."

What the hell was he supposed to do with that?

Darren had always insisted on knowing when he was going to meetings.

He'd kept an annoying little calendar for Cole to mark his meetings down in. Sometimes, Cole would write down that he'd gone to one when he hadn't. Sometimes, he went to the bar instead.

After Darren left, he'd been more motivated to actually work the steps. Now, with Noah in his life, he felt as though he could actually do this and become a sober alcoholic.

"I'm going to open up the floor for sharing."

Cole stopped his foot from tapping and set it on the floor.

"Hi, my name is Cole and I'm an alcoholic. I'm starting from square one again."

"Hi, Cole."

He leaned back in his chair. "I have a new boyfriend. A guy I've known for years. A guy I grew up with. We fell out when he found out I was gay. We recently reconnected.

"In a big way."

That received a round of laughter.

Cole folded his hands in his lap. "It caught him by surprise, my alcoholism. The last time we saw each other, we were 17. I hadn't started my drinking career yet.

"So … as of today, I'm more motivated than I've ever been. My boyfriend and I were in love twenty years ago. We still are now. He's always been the best thing in my life. He's still my best friend. He's my everything. My forever. I hope I do it … but this time I'm doing it for me."

Cole cleared his throat. "So that's my share."

"Thank you, Cole."

The rest of the meeting held Cole's interest. So many stories. So much pain. Then every once in a while … pure joy from being in recovery. Hearing how people's lives had changed for the better was inspiring. He left the building feeling lighter than he had in months.

He ducked into a coffee shop near the meeting. A few people from the meeting filtered in. He looked down at his phone. He was meeting someone. He didn't want to get into a chatting situation.

Cole: *<Hey, babe.>*

Noah: *<Hey.>*

Cole: *<I miss you.>*

Noah: *<I miss you too.>*

Cole: *<Especially that sweet little ass of yours.>*

Noah: *<It's not so little.>*

Cole: *<I know. I just want to bite a piece out of it.>*

Noah: <Maybe I'll let you bite it.>
Cole: <Is that an invitation?>
"Cole."

Cole looked up and jumped to his feet. He gave the large man he'd known for over four years a long, tight hug. He'd met Randy through a close friend. Randy had been looking for something casual and Cole had been all over it. Randy had been his first open date.

Cole sat back in his chair. He held up one finger. "Just give me one sec." He looked down at his phone. Noah had typed *yes* in response to his question of an invitation to bite his ass.

Cole smiled.

Cole: <Gotta go. My coffee date is here.>
Noah: <One of your guys?>
Cole: <Yeah. I'll call you after. Might need an emotion debrief.>
Noah: <Good luck. Love you.>
Cole: <To the moon and back.>

Cole turned his phone over and set it on the table.

"Okay, my attention is all yours."

"Work?" Randy pointed at Cole's phone.

"No …." Cole tapped the back of his phone. "Boyfriend."

Randy leaned back and crossed his arms.

"Is it serious?"

Cole nodded. "Very. He's someone I never thought would be mine. And now that he is, we never want to let each other go. This is forever. I can feel it."

Randy sighed. "I'm happy for you." His gaze wandered over Cole's body, then back to his eyes. "Does that mean we're over? Or is this guy willing to keep it open?"

"He doesn't want it to be open." Cole folded his hands on the table. "Neither do I."

"So, that's it." Randy held up both hands as if it was a question. "We're done?"

"It's been fun, it really has. We've had some good times, you and I."

Randy leaned on the table and reached for Cole's arm. He brushed his fingers over Cole's skin. "One last time … for old time's sake. You know I can make you scream."

Cole cleared his throat. "Love the screaming bit. Hoping to get it from my boyfriend, though."

"I can make you feel really good."

Cole jerked his arm away. "It's a big *no*, Randy."

Randy smiled. "Thought I'd offer."

"Offer appreciated but rejected."

"You think this boyfriend of yours can really make you cum as hard as I can?"

"Yes … and he has."

Randy made a tsking sound. "You've made up your mind."

"He's my forever guy."

Randy rose to his feet. "I really am happy for you, Cole." He stroked his fingers down Cole's cheek as he passed by him. "Say hello to Trixie for me. Maybe I'll buy her a drink sometime."

Cole held his tongue. He didn't want to get into a big discussion with Randy about Trixie not drinking anymore. The guy was walking away on good terms. Best to leave it alone.

He turned back to his phone.

Cole: <I did it. I told him it's over.>

Noah: <How did he take it?>

Cole: <He wanted one last go with me.>

There was a long pause.

Noah: <You're mine now.>

Cole: <And always will be.>

Cole tapped his finger on the screen.

Cole: <The 12-step meeting was good.>

Noah: <Did you get lots out of it?>

Cole: <I shared. It felt good.>

Noah: <So proud but I have a client coming into my office in a minute.>

Cole: <You'll come to see me at the bar tonight?>

Noah: <8:30.>

Cole: <I'll see you then. XOXO>

He waited but there was no more. He slipped his phone back in his shoulder bag. As Cole stood, his phone dinged. He dug it out and grinned as he read the message.

Noah: <More than there are grains of sand.>

Cole: <On earth and the moon.>

Cole couldn't wipe the grin off his face as he walked home. The world seemed limitless. He was in love with the most incredible man. A man who loved and supported him.

"Faggot." A car whistled by.

Cole just laughed. So what if he was? Anyone would be lucky to have the kind of love he and Noah shared. One stupid homophobe was not going to destroy his good mood.

He slowed as he passed the welcome door of the liquor store. Normally, he would nip in and grab a few things to do him for the night. He stood looking in the large window at the bottles of wine. He'd dumped all of the alcohol in his apartment down the sink after Noah left.

A corkscrew burrowed up through his chest.

Just one last bottle.

He looked down at his phone, then dug around in his bag for the list of numbers that had been passed around at the meeting. He pulled out the pink folded paper and picked a number.

"Hello."

"Hi, it's Cole. I was at the meeting this morning."

"Hey, Cole. What's up?"

"I'm standing outside a liquor store. My mind is trying to tell me I can handle one last bottle."

"Okay, play it through. You buy the bottle. You take it

home. You drink it. What happens after that? How are you going to feel?"

"Happy."

A soft laugh through the phone. "Yeah, okay, but after the alcohol wears off."

Cole blew out a long breath. "I'm gonna feel like shit."

"What else is there in your life that makes you happy?"

That was easy.

"My boyfriend."

"Happier than alcohol?"

Cole turned and leaned against the window of the liquor store. "Infinitely."

"Then what's your choice going to be? And remember, you're doing this for you."

"I'm *not* going to buy the bottle."

"One day at a time, Cole. One decision at a time. Always play it through."

Cole started walking. He didn't even look back. "Thank you for talking me off a ledge."

"That was all you."

"Regardless … thank you for taking my call."

"Anytime."

"Bye." Cole disconnected the call. He added the number to his contacts. He checked the list to see what the guy's name was. Carl. He'd have to look for him at the next meeting.

He still had hours before he had to start his drag makeup. Maybe Noah would be interested in a late lunch. He hailed a cab and arrived downtown fifteen minutes later. It felt strange going into the building with Noah's lawyer's office, not as a client but as Noah's boyfriend.

He sat on a bench seat in the lobby.

Cole: <I'm downstairs. Have you gone for lunch yet?>

Noah: <Haven't had time. What are you doing downstairs?>

Cole: <I wanted to see you. But I didn't want to barge right in.>

Cole leaned against the towering marble wall and waited. He wasn't sure if Noah would come down or ask him to come up. It would depend on how much he'd told his coworkers.

He looked at his clothes.

Gay!

Right down to his turquoise heels. Maybe Noah would be embarrassed to have him meet the people he worked with. Drag queen by night. Flamboyant queen by day.

Noah: <Come up.>

Cole leaped to his feet. His heart rate ticked up a few notches. Did this mean Noah had told everyone? He crowded into the busy elevator and checked his mascara and eyeliner in the mirrored wall beside him. His lipstick needed touched up. He was quick about it.

He dipped his brows.

Maybe he shouldn't have done that.

He started to second-guess his decision to surprise Noah. He could've waited until he was having more of a boy day. He gazed at his hand. He'd even put on long nails after Noah left.

He was going to make an excuse and ride the elevator back down. He'd be seeing Noah tonight at the bar anyway. See him on more familiar ground. He felt good about the decision.

The doors opened and Noah stepped forward in the foyer. The sweetest smile spread across Noah's face when he saw Cole.

Pure love.

No one had ever looked at Cole that way before.

Change of plan.

Cole headed straight for him.

"Hey, babe," Cole said.

Noah chewed on his bottom lip as his gaze wandered. "God, you're beautiful."

"I hope that's a good thing today."

"I don't honestly care what anyone else thinks as long as I can have you all to myself."

Cole smiled. "That can be arranged."

"Come on." Noah reached for Cole's hand. His grip was firm. "I'll introduce you to Ted."

They headed through the doors of the firm and past the receptionist. Noah dipped back and leaned on the receptionist's desk. "Linda." He pointed at Cole. "This is Cole. My boyfriend."

"Linda." Cole nodded his head.

"Nice to meet you, Cole."

They forged on.

It was exhilarating. Every person they passed, Noah introduced him to them. Some looked confused. Some happy. Some indifferent. The only thing he cared about—Noah was giddy.

And proud.

Noah rapped on a door with the name Theodore McAllister on the nameplate. A grunted, "Come in," was enough for Noah to open the door and step inside with Cole in tow.

Noah skidded to a stop.

"Dad?"

A man was standing in front of the desk of another man. The man standing turned and looked at Noah. Cole recognized that face. He'd seen it a few times when he went to Noah's house.

His childhood rushed back.

Suddenly, he was a kid again.

"Noah. I'm just having a chat with Ted. I was going to come to your office next." Noah's dad furrowed his eyebrows as he examined Cole. "Who's this?"

Cole expected Noah to drop his hand—he didn't.

"You remember Cole, Dad."

"Right." His dad nodded his head. "The Harrison kid."

"He was my best friend, Dad."

"Mr. Larkin, sir," Cole said. "Nice to see you again."

Mr. Larkin's gaze roved over Cole. Cole swallowed. Maybe the short black skirt and see-through top were a bad fashion choice to run into your boyfriend's dad with after so many years.

Mr. Larkin waved his finger at Cole. "I see you haven't changed." Then his gaze landed on where Noah was clutching Cole's hand. You could actually see the anger roll through him.

"A word, Noah."

"Not without Cole."

"Fine." Mr. Larkin grunted. "I always knew this boy would make trouble for you."

"Hardly a boy."

"Hardly a man either."

Noah surged forward, hauling Cole with him. "You have no idea what you're talking about."

Cole jerked on Noah's hand. "It's all right."

Noah looked at Cole. "No, it's not." He turned back to his dad. "I love this *man*."

Mr. Larkin honestly sputtered.

Cole had to hide a smile behind his hand. It wasn't funny but the whole scene was making him uncomfortable. Much to his horror, sometimes he laughed when he was nervous.

"Is this why you wouldn't marry Cynthia?"

Who's Cynthia?

Cole yanked on Noah's arm.

"I'll explain later," Noah said to Cole, then glared at his dad. "I told you, the reason for not marrying her would make you upset."

"But being gay. We raised you better than that?"

Cole hiccuped and covered his mouth. Okay, that was funny. That's exactly what Noah said he'd say. He felt like he needed to speak. "Mr. Larkin, I'm in love with your son. Have been since we were fourteen. Life tore us apart ... but it won't be doing that again. No matter what you say."

Noah smiled at Cole and nudged him with his shoulder.

"That's the truth," Noah said. "Neither one of us is going anywhere."

Mr. Larkin released a noncommittal sound. "You'll have to tell your mother. I'm not doing it. And your sister ... and your brother."

"That's it?" Noah asked. "No lecture?"

"Why? You're a grown man. You've made up your mind."

"You sure let me have it when I refused to marry Cynthia."

"And look what happened. You took off on us. I regret that."

"So, we're good."

"To be honest, your mother is going to be thrilled. She always loved Cole and she suspected something was going on between the two of you. I can't say I'm not surprised, though. I am. And I'm disappointed." Mr. Larkin heaved out a sigh. "I never would have suspected you were gay, but if this is the way you want to live your life, I'm not going to stand in your way."

Partial acceptance. That was a good starting place.

"Thank you, Dad. I appreciate that. We both do."

Cole felt the weight lift off Noah. The relief radiated off him. Noah lifted Cole's hand and kissed his knuckles. "Lunch?"

"Take your time," Ted said from behind Mr. Larkin. "Nice to meet you, Cole."

Cole had never been pulled out of a building quicker. And Trixie had created plenty of mayhem where she needed to be removed from a premise or two ... or five.

"I have a pasta place I want to take you to," Noah said.

"Pasta. Ugh. You're going to weigh me down."

"Then have a salad. I'm craving tortellini."

As they approached the restaurant, Noah stopped in front of the sex shop. The male mannequins with the harnesses were still in the window. He squeezed Cole's hand.

"Do you want one of those?" Cole asked.

"I don't know."

"It would give me something to hold onto when I fuck you." Noah shivered. Dirty talk definitely had a positive effect on him. "Does the thought of wearing it make you hard?"

"I wish you could feel what's going on in my pants right now."

"Then I think we should get one." Cole opened the door to the shop and strode into the cool air. Noah was hesitant and stayed close behind him. He'd probably never been in there before.

Cole went straight toward the harnesses. On the way, he spotted a couple of other things he wanted to pick up. A big fat dildo. A chunky butt plug. And some anal beads.

He handed them to Noah.

Noah looked a little shocked as he examined each package in his hands.

"You've got a hungry bottom," Cole said. "These will be fun to try."

Cole flipped through the harnesses until he found the right size. He lifted it and held it against Noah's chest to be sure of the sizing. "Maybe you can wear this to work under your shirt."

Noah audibly groaned.

That would be a yes.

Noah paid for everything which was good. Cole was once again broke. They took their bag of toys and went next door to the restaurant. As they sat and waited for their food, Cole could feel Noah's tension. His shoulders were stiff and he was answering questions with short responses.

"What's the matter?" Cole asked after far too long.

Noah stopped playing with his fork.

"This all seems to be too good to be true. Being here with you. In the real world."

"Our lives are going to unfold from here together. In the real world."

Noah tipped his head. "What does that world look like to you."

"Us together. Happy. Deeply in love."

"But do you want more than that … with me?"

Cole reached across the table and lay his hand on Noah's. "I want everything with you." He held tight to Noah's hand. "I want to marry you someday. Start a family."

Noah smiled. "The five kids?"

"And a dog."

Noah laughed. "And a dog." He leaned back in his chair. "Let's get tested."

Coal couldn't stop his eyebrows from popping up. "Tested?"

"I'd like for you to be able to fill me up. Bring us closer."

Where had that come from?

Cole cleared his throat as their food was placed on their table. He waited for the server to say her piece and move on. "I've never done that before," he said to Cole.

"We can have a first together."

"I love that … our own first." Cole lifted his phone. "I'll make the appointments."

He opened the health authority app on his phone and entered their personal information. Two weeks from now, they'd know even more about each other.

Lunch was animated as Cole detailed some of his Trixie escapades. Numbers that had taken the crowd by storm. Ones that had been embarrassing flops. Broken shoes and slipped wigs when she started out. Absolute fiascos of banter that Cole couldn't believe came out of his mouth.

Noah told him the story about Cynthia and his refusal to marry her. Cole was surprised that they'd had sex so many times. It made sense when Noah told him how uncomfortable it was. Cole told him he knew where he was coming from, having been in threesomes with straight couples.

Noah was a little shocked by that admission. They also dove into Cole's relationship with men outside his marriage. How they really had been opportunities to get away from Darren and be treated like a worthy and capable human being. Also, they'd helped him when Darren moved on.

"How many do you have left ... to tell about us?" Noah asked.

"Just two. I never liked to be dating more than three men at once. Too time-consuming."

Noah shook his head. "I don't know how you did it. Didn't you feel like you were being used?"

"Used? No one ever used me. Those men respect me."

"I'm sorry. I didn't mean to offend you. Just can't wrap my head around it."

"And you don't have to. It's over. We're together now ... just us."

Noah patted Cole's hand.

"Did you drive here?"

"No, I cabbed."

"Let me give you a ride home."

"You'll be late getting back to work."

Noah lifted the sex shop bag off the floor from under the table. "I wouldn't be able to get any work done while thinking about what you're going to do to me with these."

Cole grinned.

"Let's find out."

Chapter Ten | Noah

Noah looked up from his place on the sofa, book in hand when the front door of his house opened. Cole had a key. He'd had it for months. They spent most of their time at Noah's place. Cole used his apartment like a big closet. Even his main bedroom was showing signs of invasion.

"Hey, babe," Cole called from the front hall. "I'm home."

Noah laughed. "Kinda guessed that after the hey, babe." He loved that Cole considered this house their home. Cole clambered into the kitchen and set a bunch of grocery bags on the counter.

He bounded into the attached living room.

Noah had trouble tracking Cole's hands, he was jumping around so much. He had a metal disc gripped tightly in his fingers. "Is that what I think it is?"

Noah rose to his feet.

"6 months, baby ... I made it 6 months!"

Noah swept Cole into his arms. "Oh, my god ... so proud of you. I didn't know that was today."

"I wanted to surprise you."

Speaking of surprises, Noah had a big one for Cole. He'd been planning it for weeks. He wanted to get it right. He just needed to keep Cole out of the bedroom until he was ready.

But first, he had other news.

"We sent off the paperwork to probate your dad's will today. Nothing else left to do with the estate other than wait. It could take a few months, but there's no rush."

"Sweet!" Cole cupped Noah's face. "And thank you for

helping me get all of that other stuff out of the way. Government agencies have been notified. Pensions transferred."

"And the renter of your parents' house seems to be a nice family."

"Yeah." Cole looked wistful. "They'll be able to make memories of their own there."

Noah gave Cole a quick kiss. "I'm going to go change."

He'd deliberately left his work clothes on so he would have a reason to go into the bedroom. Once he was in there, he hauled out the bag of candles he had picked up. He placed them around the room and lit them. The chocolate-covered strawberries were on the bedside.

"What's all this?"

Noah turned to the sound of Cole's voice and smiled.

"Our missed first time ... recreated."

Cole strolled into the room, his hands over his mouth. "You didn't ...." His eyes were tearing up. "This is so sweet." He walked into Noah's open arms, then jerked back.

"What?"

"We would have been more nervous."

Noah licked his lips. "My parents are out for the night."

Cole took a step toward Noah. "Are you sure they're not coming back?"

"They'll be out until late."

"What if they catch us?"

"They won't." Noah closed the distance between them and cupped Cole's face. He breathed across Cole's lips. "I love you."

Cole's breath hitched. "I love you too."

The kiss that followed took Noah right back to his old bedroom. They were really there. His best friend was kissing him amongst his model planes, soccer balls, and band posters.

Cole wrapped his arms around Noah's neck and deepened

the kiss. Noah groaned and grabbed Cole's hips, stepped closer, and pressed his cock against Cole's.

They were both hard.

Cole broke from the kiss. "Your sister might hear us."

"My sister doesn't care. She's with her boyfriend."

"Your brother?" Cole gasped as Noah cupped his cock in one hand.

"Out at a friend's overnight." Noah rubbed the length of Cole's cock through his pants. He descended on Cole's mouth and slipped his tongue between his lips. The taste, as always, was intoxicating. He imagined it being the first time he had kissed Cole like that.

Cole's fingers became busy undoing Noah's shirt. Once he had completed the row, he pushed the crisp fabric over Noah's shoulders, then stripped it off his arms.

He flung it to one side and stroked Noah's chest. The way Cole wandered over it with his fingers and his gaze, it felt like the first time he had ever done it.

"I want to see you too," Noah whispered.

Noah helped Cole lift his shirt off over his head. He spent the next few seconds tracing his fingers along Cole's collarbones and around each nipple.

"You're beautiful."

"So are you." Cole cupped Noah's face and brought their lips back together. The connection was slow and lazy. They were in no hurry. His parents wouldn't be home for hours yet.

Noah walked Cole back toward the bed. Cole's knees met the edge of the mattress. He sat down, then fell backward, and flung his arms out to either side.

"I'm yours," Cole whispered.

"And I'm yours." Noah gently tugged Cole's pants off his hips. Cole raised his ass and Noah pulled the pants down off over his feet. He left his underwear in place.

Noah let the feeling of innocent shyness flow through him.

This was the first time for both of them.

They were in love.

Cole scrambled up in bed. He pulled back the covers and smiled.

"Oh, my god ... are these Space Wars sheets?"

Noah laughed. "You have no idea how hard it was to track those down."

Cole shook his head. "I fucking love you."

"Shh." Noah looked over his shoulder. "My sister might hear you."

"Sorry." Cole bit his bottom lip, making him look like an admonished angel. And just like that, they were back in time. Noah removed his pants and socks and climbed onto the bed.

Noah fell into Cole's arms. Their bare chests collided as they dove for each other's mouths. He slung one leg between Cole's so they could grind on each other's hips.

They humped and groaned until they were both close.

That wasn't the fantasy Noah had replayed every night for months in his young mind. He climbed off Cole and retrieved the chocolate-covered strawberries.

He started on Cole's bottom lip, then dragged the chocolaty tip down the center of Cole's chin and along his throat to the little hollow between Cole's collarbones.

He lay his lips there and licked the chocolate-scented skin.

Noah shuffled down. Cole arched his back and moaned as Noah circled each nipple with the strawberry and then his tongue. He swirled circles on Cole's skin with his tongue over Cole's ribcage and down to his belly. He pulled Cole's underwear down a little and drew a circle with the strawberry on each of Cole's hips. He sucked and kissed Cole's hips.

"Noah," Cole whispered. An exhalation.

Cole's hips rocked up as Noah nuzzled Cole's hard cock through his underwear. He mouthed and kissed it and rolled his chin across the shaft. He immersed himself in his male scent.

"Take them off." Cole's voice was quiet and strained.

Noah hooked his thumbs in the bands and pulled them slowly off Cole's body. His cock sprung free. Noah remembered what it had been like to see it for the first time.

Cole shoved the underwear off his feet.

Noah licked the strawberry. It was soft and sweet. The chocolate was melting from the heat of Cole's body. He drew a circle on the skin above Cole's shaft and licked it clean.

Around Cole's cockhead, a chocolate coating. Down his length. Across his balls. Noah started licking his balls to taste the chocolate first. Warm, wet swipes with his tongue. Up his shaft, his tongue wide and flat, and slow. He circled his tongue on Cole's cockhead. There was a heady taste of chocolate mixed with precum. He capped his mouth over the tip to chase that taste. He sucked only as far as the ridge until Cole grabbed a handful of his hair and mewled so sweetly.

He abandoned Cole's cock and kissed his way back up his body. He rubbed the tip of the strawberry on Cole's bottom lip. Cole chased after it and took a sizeable bite.

Noah wanted some of that.

He covered Cole's mouth and shared the sweet fruit, their tongues tangling, swapping its juicy flesh until they'd both swallowed pieces of it.

"These … off," Cole said against Noah's lips as he tugged on Noah's underwear.

Noah was quick to remove them.

"I want to feel you inside me," Cole said, his voice all breathy and soft.

It's the way Noah had always dreamed it would be. Cole in his bed, making love to him. In all the months they'd been together, Cole had rarely bottomed.

Now, in his adolescent bedroom, he wanted to live out his fantasy.

Cole was right there with him.

It's the way it would have happened.

Cole cupped Noah's face and wrapped his legs around Noah's hips.

"You're mine," Cole whispered and took Noah's mouth. Gasps and sighs followed as their lips caressed and devoured. With one hand beside Cole's shoulder, Noah managed to angle his body, pop the cap of the lube with one hand, and spill a stream of it onto his bare cock. They hadn't used condoms in months. Most mornings evidence of their lovemaking would be painting his hole.

He flung the lube aside and coated his cock in it. Cole didn't like any prepping done on his ass. He liked to feel the full burn. It was doubtful they would have done it any differently if it was their first time. They would have been too anxious to get to the main attraction.

Noah pushed his cockhead past Cole's tight ring. His heart thundered. The wail from Cole was loud and agonizingly carnal. It turned into a guttural scream every time Noah glided forward.

His sister would have heard that for sure.

He closed in against Cole's body.

"You okay, babe?" Noah asked. Cole's eyes were watering. The best Cole could do was nod and suck in a shuddering breath. It would be easier for Cole now.

Noah's strokes would be slow and steady.

He pumped his hips in an easy rhythm, watching every change in Cole's face—in his eyes—with his lips. He wanted to catch every little nuance of Cole's pleasure. Every shiver. Every shudder. Every sigh and gasp. Every flutter of his thick eyelashes.

He couldn't ignore the breathy moans. He needed to feel them in his throat. Noah closed his mouth over Cole's, kissing him. Every thrust pushed sound from Cole's chest.

Is this what it would have been like?

Noah liked to think so.

Their love was so profound that anything they did together would have been heaven. Even if they'd been clumsy and awkward. It would have been perfect.

Cole clung to Noah's bottom lip with his teeth.

He gasped and tipped his head back. "Cumming."

Every shudder of Cole's body as he spilled between them, tightened his body's grip on Noah's cock. Noah bent a knee and rode higher into Cole, rocking him into the bedding.

He nearly swore but he wanted to keep it clean and pure.

Like their love.

He climaxed deep inside Cole, flooding him. And then just lay there on top of him, basking in the moments they had shared while recreating their first time.

Cole shifted beneath him. "Something is under my head. This pillow is lumpy."

Noah stopped Cole from digging around underneath it.

"Don't. Not yet." Noah pulled away from Cole, then straddled his hips. He leaned forward, fished around under the pillow, and pulled out a small blue velvet box.

Cole grasped Noah's thighs and dug his nails in. "You didn't."

"I did." Noah grinned.

"Now?"

Noah laughed. "No, tomorrow." He popped open the box. "No, I'm asking you today."

A silver band encrusted with diamonds, illuminated by the candlelight, sparkled from within the box. Cole reached forward and touched it. "It's real. You're really asking me."

"I'm really asking you."

Cole covered his mouth, containing a little squeal as he drummed his legs up and down, jostling Noah. "And I'm really saying yes."

Noah set the box on Cole's chest.

Somewhere inside, Noah was in shock. His best friend in the world had said yes to marrying him. It was beyond any of his childhood fantasies. This was here—this was now.

He lifted the ring from the box. Cole was staring up at him, his gorgeous emerald eyes outshining anything the diamonds were throwing out at them.

"I put this ring on your finger and I'm yours forever," Noah said.

Cole held up his left hand. "And I'm yours."

The ring slipped on as if it was always meant to be there. As though their lives were meant to be entwined. This was forever. They would never be without each other again.

Dear Reader

I hope you enjoyed reading *Drag Undivided*.

Please take a moment to review this book on the website of the store where you purchased your copy of *Drag Undivided*.

If you would like to touch base and say hello to the author, you can email them at: leigh@leighjarrett.com

About the Author

Leigh Jarrett (she/he) is an unabashedly queer, quirky, and passionate author of Contemporary MM+ Romantic Fiction. Their published contemporary works include warm and always sexy HEA romances as well as dark romances filled with grit, trauma, and angst.

In their hometown of Victoria, BC, Canada, Leigh can be found nestled up with their fabulously supportive wife and trusty laptop or enjoying the wondrous Vancouver Island outdoors.

Please consider subscribing to Leigh's newsletter to stay up to date with their new releases and promos. If you're interested in MM+ Fantasy and Paranormal Romance, check out one of Leigh's other pen names, JT Fader, on their JT Fader Fantasticals website and newsletter jtfader.com.

To connect with Leigh Jarrett:

Email: leigh@leighjarrett.com

Website and newsletter: leighjarrett.com

You can also find Leigh on Bluesky

Other Books by Leigh Jarrett

"It all came down to a matter of trust."
A Friends to Lovers M/M Gay Romance
Snowblind

"Find love in the least expected place."
An Enemies to Lovers M/M Gay Romance

Merlot Rebellion

"Risking it all to follow your heart."
A Found Family M/M Bisexual Romance

Capital Adoration

"Brave enough to pursue love."
An Age Gap M/M Gay Romance

Pacific Pursuit

"Learning a new path to love."
A Roommates to Lovers Bisexual Awakening M/M Romance

Academic Adoration

"Strumming your way to love."
A Grumpy/Sunshine Gay Awakening M/M Romance

Rhythmic Bliss

www.ingramcontent.com/pod-product-compliance
Lightning Source LLC
Chambersburg PA
CBHW070338130626
46556CB00007B/2925